W9-CIM-211

NOCTURNES

by the same author

A PALE VIEW OF HILLS
AN ARTIST OF THE FLOATING WORLD
THE REMAINS OF THE DAY
THE UNCONSOLED
WHEN WE WERE ORPHANS
NEVER LET ME GO

NOCTURNES

Five Stories of Music and Nightfall

Kazuo Ishiguro

Alfred A. Knopf Canada

PUBLISHED BY ALFRED A. KNOPF CANADA

Copyright © 2009 Kazuo Ishiguro

All rights reserved under International and Pan-American Copyright
Conventions. No part of this book may be reproduced in any form or by any
electronic or mechanical means, including information storage and retrieval
systems, without permission in writing from the publisher, except by a
reviewer, who may quote brief passages in a review. Published in 2009 by
Alfred A. Knopf Canada, a division of Random House of Canada Limited.
Distributed by Random House of Canada Limited, Toronto.

Knopf Canada and colophon are trademarks.

www.randomhouse.ca

Library and Archives Canada Cataloguing in Publication

Ishiguro, Kazuo, 1954–
Nocturnes : five stories of music and nightfall / Kazuo Ishiguro.

ISBN 978-0-307-39787-4

I. Title.

PR6059.S5N62 2009   823'.914   C2008-907092-5

Typeset by Faber and Faber Ltd.

First Edition

Printed and bound in the United States of America

2 4 6 8 10 9 7 5 3 1

For Deborah Rogers

Contents

CROONER

THE MORNING I spotted Tony Gardner sitting among the tourists, spring was just arriving here in Venice. We'd completed our first full week outside in the piazza – a relief, let me tell you, after all those stuffy hours performing from the back of the cafe, getting in the way of customers wanting to use the staircase. There was quite a breeze that morning, and our brand-new marquee was flapping all around us, but we were all feeling a little bit brighter and fresher, and I guess it showed in our music.

But here I am talking like I'm a regular band member. Actually, I'm one of the 'gypsies', as the other musicians call us, one of the guys who move around the piazza, helping out whichever of the three cafe orchestras needs us. Mostly I play here at the Caffè Lavena, but on a busy afternoon, I might do a set with the Quadri boys, go over to the Florian, then back across the square to the Lavena. I get on fine with them all – and with the waiters too – and in any other city I'd have a regular position by now. But in this place, so obsessed with tradition and the past, everything's upside down. Anywhere else, being a guitar player would go in a guy's favour. But here? A guitar! The cafe managers get uneasy. It looks too modern, the tourists won't like it. Last autumn I got myself a vintage jazz model with an oval sound-hole, the kind of thing Django Reinhardt might have played, so there was no way anyone would mistake me for a rock-and-roller. That made things a little easier, but the cafe managers, they still don't like it. The truth is, if you're a guitarist, you can be Joe Pass, they still wouldn't give you a regular job in this square.

There's also, of course, the small matter of my not being Italian, never mind Venetian. It's the same for that big Czech guy with the alto sax. We're well liked, we're needed by the other musicians, but we don't quite fit the official bill. Just play and keep your mouth shut, that's what the cafe managers always say. That way the tourists won't know you're not Italian. Wear your suit, sunglasses, keep the hair combed back, no one will know the difference, just don't start talking.

But I don't do too bad. All three cafe orchestras, especially when they have to play at the same time from their rival tents, they need a guitar – something soft, solid, but amplified, thumping out the chords from the back. I guess you're thinking, three bands playing at the same time in the same square, that would sound like a real mess. But the Piazza San Marco's big enough to take it. A tourist strolling across the square will hear one tune fade out, another fade in, like he's shifting the dial on a radio. What tourists can't take too much of is the classical stuff, all these instrumental versions of famous arias. Okay, this is San Marco, they don't want the latest pop hits. But every few minutes they want something they recognise, maybe an old Julie Andrews number, or the theme from a famous movie. I remember once last summer, going from band to band and playing 'The Godfather' nine times in one afternoon.

Anyway there we were that spring morning, playing in front of a good crowd of tourists, when I saw Tony Gardner, sitting alone with his coffee, almost directly in front of us, maybe six metres back from our marquee. We get famous people in the square all the time, we never make a fuss. At the end of a number, maybe a quiet word will go around the band members. Look, there's Warren Beatty. Look, it's Kissinger. That woman, she's the one who was in the movie about the men who swap their faces. We're used to it. This is the Piazza San Marco after all. But when I realised it was Tony Gardner sitting there, that was different. I *did* get excited.

Tony Gardner had been my mother's favourite. Back home, back in the communist days, it had been really hard to get records like that, but my mother had pretty much his whole collection. Once when I was a boy, I scratched one of those precious records. The apartment was so cramped, and a boy my age, you just had to move around sometimes, especially during those cold months when you couldn't go outside. So I was playing this game jumping from our little sofa to the armchair, and one time I misjudged it and hit the record player. The needle went across the record with a zip – this was long before CDs – and my mother came in from the kitchen and began shouting at me. I felt so bad, not just because she was shouting at me, but because I knew it was one of Tony Gardner's records, and I knew how much it meant to her. And I knew that this one too would now have those popping noises going through it while he crooned those American songs. Years later, when I was working in Warsaw and I got to know about black-market records, I gave my mother replacements of all her worn-out Tony Gardner albums, including that one I scratched. It took me over three years, but I kept getting them, one by one, and each time I went back to see her I'd bring her another.

So you see why I got so excited when I recognised him, barely six metres away. At first I couldn't quite believe it, and I might have been a beat late with a chord change. Tony Gardner! What would my dear mother have said if she'd known! For her sake, for the sake of her memory, I had to go and say something to him, never mind if the other musicians laughed and said I was acting like a bell-boy.

But of course I couldn't just rush over to him, pushing aside the tables and chairs. There was our set to finish. It was agony, I can tell you, another three, four numbers, and every second I thought he was about to get up and walk off. But he kept sitting there, by himself, staring into his coffee, stirring it like he was really puzzled by what the waiter had brought him. He looked like any other American tourist, dressed in a pale-blue polo shirt and loose grey trousers. His hair, very dark, very shiny on those record covers, was almost white now, but there was still plenty of it, and it was immaculately groomed in the same style he'd had back then. When I'd first spotted him, he'd had his dark glasses in his hand – I doubt if I'd have recognised him otherwise – but as our set went on and I kept watching him, he put

them on his face, took them off again, then back on again.
He looked preoccupied and it disappointed me to see he
wasn't really listening to our music.

Then our set was over. I hurried out of the tent without
saying anything to the others, made my way to Tony
Gardner's table, then had a moment's panic not knowing
how to start the conversation. I was standing behind him,
but some sixth sense made him turn and look up at me – I
guess it was all those years of having fans come up to him
– and next thing I was introducing myself, explaining how
much I admired him, how I was in the band he'd just been
listening to, how my mother had been such a fan, all in one
big rush. He listened with a grave expression, nodding
every few seconds like he was my doctor. I kept talking and
all he said every now and then was: 'Is that so?' After a
while I thought it was time to leave and I'd started to move
away when he said:

'So you come from one of those communist countries.
That must have been tough.'

'That's all in the past.' I did a cheerful shrug. 'We're a
free country now. A democracy.'

'That's good to hear. And that was your crew playing for
us just now. Sit down. You want some coffee?'

I told him I didn't want to impose, but there was now
something gently insistent about Mr Gardner. 'No, no, sit
down. Your mother liked my records, you were saying.'

So I sat down and told him some more. About my
mother, our apartment, the black-market records. And
though I couldn't remember what the albums were called,
I started describing the pictures on their sleeves the way I

remembered them, and each time I did this, he'd put his finger up in the air and say something like: 'Oh, that would be *Inimitable. The Inimitable Tony Gardner.*' I think we were both really enjoying this game, but then I noticed Mr Gardner's gaze move off me, and I turned just in time to see a woman coming up to our table.

She was one of those American ladies who are so classy, with great hair, clothes and figure, you don't realise they're not so young until you see them up close. Far away, I might have mistaken her for a model out of those glossy fashion magazines. But when she sat down next to Mr Gardner and pushed her dark glasses onto her forehead, I realised she must be at least fifty, maybe more. Mr Gardner said to me: 'This is Lindy, my wife.'

Mrs Gardner flashed me a smile that was kind of forced, then said to her husband: 'So who's this? You've made yourself a friend.'

'That's right, honey. I was having a good time talking here with . . . I'm sorry, friend, I don't know your name.'

'Jan,' I said quickly. 'But friends call me Janeck.'

Lindy Gardner said: 'You mean your nickname's longer than your real name? How does that work?'

'Don't be rude to the man, honey.'

'I'm not being rude.'

'Don't make fun of the man's name, honey. That's a good girl.'

Lindy Gardner turned to me with a helpless sort of expression. 'You know what he's talking about? Did I insult you?'

'No, no,' I said, 'not at all, Mrs Gardner.'

[8]

'He's always telling me I'm rude to the public. But I'm not rude. Was I rude to you just now?' Then to Mr Gardner: 'I speak to the public in a *natural* way, sweetie. It's *my* way. I'm never rude.'

'Okay, honey,' Mr Gardner said, 'let's not make a big thing of it. Anyhow, this man here, he's not the public.'

'Oh, he's not? Then what is he? A long-lost nephew?'

'Be nice, honey. This man, he's a colleague. A musician, a pro. He's just been entertaining us all.' He gestured towards our marquee.

'Oh right!' Lindy Gardner turned to me again. 'You were playing up there just now? Well, that was pretty. You were on the accordion, right? Real pretty!'

'Thank you very much. Actually, I'm the guitarist.'

'Guitarist? You're kidding me. I was watching you only a minute ago. Sitting right there, next to the double bass man, playing so beautifully on your accordion.'

'Pardon me, that was in fact Carlo on the accordion. The big bald guy . . .'

'Are you sure? You're not kidding me?'

'Honey, I've told you. Don't be rude to the man.'

He hadn't shouted exactly, but his voice was suddenly hard and angry, and now there was a strange silence. Then Mr Gardner himself broke it, saying gently:

'I'm sorry, honey. I didn't mean to snap at you.'

He reached out a hand and grasped one of hers. I'd kind of expected her to shake him off, but instead, she moved in her chair so she was closer to him, and put her free hand over their clasped pair. They sat there like that for a few seconds, Mr Gardner, his head bowed, his wife gazing emptily past his shoulder, across the square towards the Basilica, though her eyes didn't seem to be seeing anything. For those few moments it was like they'd forgotten not just me sitting with them, but all the people in the piazza. Then she said, almost in a whisper:

'That's okay, sweetie. It was my fault. Getting you all upset.'

They went on sitting like that a little longer, their hands locked. Then she sighed, let go of Mr Gardner and looked at me. She'd looked at me before, but this time it was different. This time I could feel her charm. It was like she had this dial, going zero to ten, and with me, at that moment, she'd decided to turn it to six or seven, but I could feel it really strong, and if she'd asked some favour of me – if say she'd asked me to go across the square and buy her some flowers – I'd have done it happily.

'Janeck,' she said. 'That's your name, right? I'm sorry, Janeck. Tony's right. I'd no business speaking to you the way I did.'

'Mrs Gardner, really, please don't worry . . .'

'And I disturbed the two of you talking. Musicians' talk, I bet. You know what? I'm gonna leave the two of you to get on with it.'

'No reason to go, honey,' Mr Gardner said.

'Oh yes there is, sweetie. I'm absolutely *yearning* to go look in that Prada store. I only came over just now to tell you I'd be longer than I said.'

'Okay, honey.' Tony Gardner straightened for the first time and took a deep breath. 'So long as you're sure you're happy doing that.'

'I'm gonna have a fantastic time in that store. So you two fellas, you have yourselves a good talk.' She got to her feet and touched me on the shoulder. 'You take care, Janeck.'

We watched her walk away, then Mr Gardner asked me a few things about being a musician in Venice, and about the Quadri orchestra in particular, who'd started playing just at that moment. He didn't seem to listen so carefully to my answers and I was about to excuse myself and leave, when he said suddenly:

'There's something I want to put to you, friend. Let me tell you what's on my mind and you can turn me down if that's what you want.' He leaned forward and lowered his voice. 'Can I tell you something? The first time Lindy and I came here to Venice, it was our honeymoon. Twenty-seven years ago. And for all our happy memories of this place, we'd never been back, not together anyway. So when we were planning this trip, this special trip of ours, we said to ourselves we've got to spend a few days in Venice.'

'It's your anniversary, Mr Gardner?'

'Anniversary?' He looked startled.

'I'm sorry,' I said. 'I just thought, because you said this was your special trip.'

He went on looking startled for a while, then he laughed, a big, booming laugh, and suddenly I remembered this particular song my mother used to play all the time where he does a talking passage in the middle of the song, something about not caring that this woman has left him, and he does this sardonic laugh. Now the same laugh was booming across the square. Then he said:

'Anniversary? No, no, it's not our anniversary. But what I'm proposing, it's not so far off. Because I want to do something very romantic. I want to serenade her. Properly, Venice style. That's where you come in. You play your guitar, I sing. We do it from a gondola, we drift under the window, I sing up to her. We're renting a palazzo not far from here. The bedroom window looks over the canal. After dark, it'll be perfect. The lamps on the walls light things up just right. You and me in a gondola, she comes to the window. All her favourite numbers. We don't need to do it for long, the evenings are still kinda chilly. Just three or four songs, that's what I have in mind. I'll see you're well compensated. What do you say?'

'Mr Gardner, I'd be absolutely honoured. As I told you, you've been an important figure for me. When were you thinking of doing this?'

'If it doesn't rain, why not tonight? Around eight-thirty? We eat dinner early, so we'll be back by then. I'll make some excuse, leave the apartment, come and meet you. I'll have a gondola fixed up, we'll come back along the canal, stop under the window. It'll be perfect. What do you say?'

You can probably imagine, this was like a dream come true. And besides, it seemed such a sweet idea, this couple – he in his sixties, she in her fifties – behaving like teenagers in love. In fact it was so sweet an idea it almost, but not quite, made me forget the scene I'd just witnessed between them. What I mean is, even at that stage, I knew deep down that things wouldn't be as straightforward as he was making out.

For the next few minutes Mr Gardner and I sat there

discussing all the details – which songs he wanted, the keys he preferred, all those kinds of things. Then it was time for me to get back to the marquee and our next set, so I stood up, shook his hand and told him he could absolutely count on me that evening.

The streets were dark and quiet as I went to meet Mr Gardner that night. In those days I'd always get lost whenever I moved much beyond the Piazza San Marco, so even though I'd allowed myself plenty of time, even though I knew the little bridge where Mr Gardner had told me to be, I was still a few minutes late.

He was standing right under a lamp, wearing a crumpled dark suit, and his shirt was open down to the third or fourth button, so you could see the hairs on his chest. When I apologised for being late, he said:

'What's a few minutes? Lindy and I have been married twenty-seven years. What's a few minutes?'

He wasn't angry, but his mood seemed grave and solemn – not at all romantic. Behind him was the gondola, gently rocking in the water, and I saw the gondolier was Vittorio, a guy I don't like much. To my face, Vittorio's always friendly, but I know – I knew back then – he goes around saying all kinds of foul things, all of it rubbish, about people like me, people he calls 'the foreigners from the new countries'. That's why, when he greeted me that evening like a brother, I just nodded, and waited silently while he helped Mr Gardner into the gondola. Then I passed him my guitar – I'd brought my Spanish guitar, not the one with the oval sound-hole – and got in myself.

Mr Gardner kept shifting positions at the front of the boat, and at one point sat down so heavily we nearly capsized. But he didn't seem to notice and as we pushed off, he kept staring into the water.

For a few minutes we drifted in silence, past dark buildings and under low bridges. Then he came out of his deep thoughts and said:

'Listen, friend. I know we agreed on a set for this evening. But I've been thinking. Lindy loves that song, "By the Time I Get to Phoenix". I recorded it once a long time ago.'

'Sure, Mr Gardner. My mother always said your version was better than Sinatra's. Or that famous one by Glenn Campbell.'

Mr Gardner nodded, then I couldn't see his face for a while. Vittorio sent his gondolier's cry echoing around the walls before steering us round a corner.

'I used to sing it to her a lot,' Mr Gardner said. 'You know, I think she'd like to hear it tonight. You're familiar with the tune?'

My guitar was out of the case by this time, so I played a few bars of the song.

'Take it up,' he said. 'Up to E-flat. That's how I did it on the album.'

So I played the chords in that key, and after maybe a whole verse had gone by, Mr Gardner began to sing, very softly, under his breath, like he could only half remember the words. But his voice resonated well in that quiet canal. In fact, it sounded really beautiful. And for a moment it was like I was a boy again, back in that apartment, lying on the carpet while my mother sat on the sofa, exhausted, or maybe heartbroken, while Tony Gardner's album spun in the corner of the room.

Mr Gardner broke off suddenly and said: 'Okay. We'll do "Phoenix" in E-flat. Then maybe "I Fall in Love Too Easily", like we planned. And we'll finish with "One for My Baby". That'll be enough. She won't listen to any more than that.'

He seemed to sink back into his thoughts after that, and we drifted along through the darkness to the sound of Vittorio's gentle splashes.

'Mr Gardner,' I said eventually, 'I hope you don't mind me asking. But is Mrs Gardner expecting this recital? Or is this going to be a wonderful surprise?'

He sighed heavily, then said: 'I guess we'd have to put this in the wonderful surprise category.' Then he added: 'Lord knows how she'll react. We might not make it all the way to "One for My Baby".'

Vittorio steered us round another corner, and suddenly there was laughter and music, and we were drifting past a large, brightly lit restaurant. Every table seemed taken, the waiters were rushing about, the diners looked very happy, even though it couldn't have been so warm next to the canal at that time of year. After the quiet and the darkness we'd been travelling through, the restaurant was kind of unsettling. It felt like we were the stationary ones, watching from the quay, as this glittering party boat slid by. I noticed a few faces look our way, but no one paid us much attention. Then the restaurant was behind us, and I said:

'It's funny. Can you imagine what those tourists would

do if they realised a boat had just gone by containing the legendary Tony Gardner?'

Vittorio, who doesn't understand much English, got the gist of this and gave a little laugh. But Mr Gardner didn't respond for some time. We were back in the dark again, going along a narrow canal past dimly lit doorways, when he said:

'My friend, you come from a communist country. That's why you don't realise how these things work.'

'Mr Gardner,' I said, 'my country isn't communist any more. We're free people now.'

'I'm sorry. I didn't mean to denigrate your nation. You're a brave people. I hope you win peace and prosperity. But what I intended to say to you, friend, what I meant was that coming from where you do, quite naturally, there are many things you don't understand yet. Just like there'd be many things I wouldn't understand in your country.'

'I guess that's right, Mr Gardner.'

'Those people we passed just now. If you'd gone up to them and said, "Hey, do any of you remember Tony Gardner?" then maybe some of them, most of them even, might have said yes. Who knows? But drifting by the way we just did, even if they'd recognised me, would they get excited? I don't think so. They wouldn't put down their forks, they wouldn't interrupt their candlelit heart-to-hearts. Why should they? Just some crooner from a bygone era.'

'I can't believe that, Mr Gardner. You're a classic. You're like Sinatra or Dean Martin. Some class acts, they never go out of fashion. Not like these pop stars.'

'You're very kind to say that, friend. I know you mean well. But tonight of all nights, it's no time to be kidding me.'

I was about to protest, but something in his manner told me to drop the whole subject. So we kept moving, no one speaking. To be honest, I was now beginning to wonder what I'd got myself into, what this whole serenade thing was about. And these were Americans, after all. For all I knew, when Mr Gardner started singing, Mrs Gardner would come to the window with a gun and fire down at us.

Maybe Vittorio's thoughts were moving along the same lines, because as we passed under a lantern on the side of a wall, he gave me a look as though to say: 'We've got a strange one here, haven't we, *amico*?' But I didn't respond. I wasn't going to side with the likes of him against Mr Gardner. According to Vittorio, foreigners like me, we go around ripping off tourists, littering the canals, in general ruining the whole damn city. Some days, if he's in a bad mood, he'll claim we're muggers – rapists, even. I asked him once to his face if it was true he was going around saying such things, and he swore it was all a pack of lies. How could he be a racist when he had a Jewish aunt he adored like a mother? But one afternoon I was killing time between sets, leaning over a bridge in Dorsoduro, and a gondola passed underneath. There were three tourists sitting in it, and Vittorio standing over them with his oar, holding forth for the world to hear, coming out with this very same rubbish. So he can meet my eye all he likes, he'll get no camaraderie from me.

'Let me tell you a little secret,' Mr Gardner said suddenly. 'A little secret about performance. One pro to another. It's quite simple. You've got to know something, doesn't matter what it is, you've got to know something about your audience. Something that for you, in your mind, distinguishes that audience from the one you sang to the night before. Let's say you're in Milwaukee. You've got to ask yourself, what's different, what's *special* about a Milwaukee audience? What makes it different from a Madison audience? Can't think of anything, you just keep on trying till you do. Milwaukee, Milwaukee. They have good pork chops in Milwaukee. That'll work, that's what you use when you step out there. You don't have to say a word about it to them, it's what's in your mind when you sing to them. These people in front of you, they're the ones who eat good pork chops. They have high standards when it comes to pork chops. You understand what I'm saying? That way the audience becomes someone you know, someone you can perform to. There, that's my secret. One pro to another.'

'Well, thank you, Mr Gardner. I'd never thought about it that way. A tip from someone like you, I won't forget it.'

'So tonight,' he went on, 'we're performing for Lindy. Lindy's the audience. So I'm going to tell you something about Lindy. You want to hear about Lindy?'

'Of course, Mr Gardner,' I said. 'I'd like to hear about her very much.'

For the next twenty minutes or so, we sat in that gondola, drifting round and round, while Mr Gardner talked.

Sometimes his voice went down to a murmur, like he was talking to himself. Other times, when a lamp or a passing window threw some light across our boat, he'd remember me, raise his voice, and say something like: 'You understand what I'm saying, friend?'

His wife, he told me, had come from a small town in Minnesota, in the middle of America, where her schoolteachers gave her a hard time because she was always looking at magazines of movie stars instead of studying.

'What these ladies never realised was that Lindy had big plans. And look at her now. Rich, beautiful, travelled all over the world. And those schoolteachers, where are they today? What kind of lives have they had? If they'd looked at a few more movie magazines, had a few more dreams, they too might have a little of what Lindy has today.'

At nineteen, she'd hitch-hiked to California, wanting to get to Hollywood. Instead, she'd found herself in the outskirts of Los Angeles, working as a waitress in a roadside diner.

'Surprising thing,' Mr Gardner said. 'This diner, this regular little place off the highway. It turned out to be the best place she could have wound up. Because this was where all the ambitious girls came in, morning till night. They used to meet there, seven, eight, a dozen of them, they'd order their coffees, their hot dogs, sit in there for hours and talk.'

These girls, all a little older than Lindy, had come from every part of America and had been in the LA area for at least two or three years. They came into the diner to swap gossip and hard-luck stories, discuss tactics, keep a check on each other's progress. But the main draw of the place was Meg, a woman in her forties, the waitress Lindy worked with.

'To these girls Meg was their big sister, their fountain of wisdom. Because once upon a time, she'd been exactly like them. You've got to understand, these were serious girls, really ambitious, determined girls. Did they talk about clothes and shoes and make-up like other girls? Sure they did. But they only talked about which clothes and shoes and make-up would help them marry a star. Did they talk about movies? Did they talk about the music scene? You bet. But they talked about which movie stars and singers were single, which ones were unhappily married, which ones were getting divorced. And Meg, you see, she could tell them all this, and much, much more. Meg had been down that road before them. She knew all the rules, all the tricks, when it came to marrying a star. And Lindy sat with them and took everything in. That little hot-dog diner was her Harvard, her Yale. A nineteen-year-old from Minnesota? Makes me shudder now to think what could have happened to her. But she got lucky.'

'Mr Gardner,' I said, 'excuse me for interrupting. But if this Meg was so wise about everything, how come she wasn't married to a star herself? Why was she serving hot dogs in this diner?'

'Good question, but you don't quite see how these things work. Okay, this lady, Meg, she hadn't made it. But the point is, she'd watched the ones who had. You understand, friend? She'd been just like those girls once, and she'd watched some succeed, others fail. She'd seen the pitfalls, she'd seen the golden stairways. She could tell them all the stories and those girls listened. And some of them learned. Lindy, for one. Like I say, that was her Harvard. It made her what she is. It gave her the strength she needed later on, and boy, did she need it. It took her six years before her first break came along. Can you imagine it? Six years of manoeuvring, planning, putting yourself on the line like that. Getting knocked back over and over again. But it's just like in our business. You can't roll over and give up after the first few knocks. The girls who do, you can see them any place, married to nobodies in nowhere towns. But just a few of them, the ones like Lindy, they learn from every knock, they come back stronger, tougher, they come back fighting and mad. You think Lindy didn't suffer humiliation? Even with her beauty and charm? What people don't realise is that beauty isn't the half of it. Use it wrong, you get treated like a whore. Anyway, after six years, she finally got her break.'

'That's when she met you, Mr Gardner?'

'Me? No, no. I didn't come on the scene for a while longer. She married Dino Hartman. You've never heard of Dino?' Mr Gardner did a slightly unkind laugh here. 'Poor Dino. I guess Dino's records wouldn't have made it to the communist countries. But Dino had quite a name for himself in those days. He sang in Vegas a lot, had a few gold records. Like I said, that was Lindy's big break. When I first met her, she was Dino's wife. Old Meg had explained that's how it happens all the time. Sure, a girl can get lucky first time, go straight to the top, marry a Sinatra or a Brando. But it doesn't usually happen like that. A girl's got to be prepared to get out of the elevator at the second floor, walk around. She needs to get used to the air on that floor. Then maybe, one day, on that second floor, she'll run into someone who's come down from the penthouse for a few minutes, maybe to fetch something. And this guy says to her, hey, how about coming back up with me, up to the top floor. Lindy knew that's how it usually played out. She wasn't weakening when she married Dino, she wasn't cutting her ambition down to size. And Dino was a decent guy. I always liked him. That's why, even though I fell badly for Lindy the moment I first saw her, I didn't make a move. I was the perfect gentleman. I found out later that was what made Lindy all the more determined. Man, you've got to admire a girl like that! I have to tell you, friend, I was a bright, bright star around this time. I guess this would be around when your mother was listening to me. Dino, though, his star was starting to go down fast. It was tough for a lot of singers just around then. Everything was changing. Kids were listening to the Beatles, the Rolling Stones. Poor Dino, he sounded too much like Bing Crosby. He tried a bossa nova album folks just laughed at. Definitely time for Lindy to get out. No one could have accused us of anything in that situation. I don't think even Dino really blamed us. So I made my move. That's how she got up to the penthouse.

'We got married in Vegas, we had the hotel fill the bathtub with champagne. That song we're gonna do tonight, "I Fall in Love Too Easily". You know why I chose that one? You want to know? We were in London once, not long after we got married. We came up to our room after breakfast and the maid's in there cleaning our suite. But Lindy and I are horny as rabbits. So we go in, and we can hear the maid vacuuming our lounge, but we can't see her, she's through the partition. So we sneak through on tip-toes, like we're kids, you know? We sneak through to the bedroom, close the door. We can see the maid's finished the bedroom already, so maybe she doesn't need to come back, but we don't know that for sure. Either way, we don't care. We tear off our clothes, we make love on the bed, and all the time the maid's on the other side, moving around our suite, no idea we've come in. I tell you, we were horny, but after a while, we found the whole thing so funny, we just kept laughing. Then we'd finished and we were lying there in each other's arms, and the maid was still out there and you know what, she starts singing! She's finished with the vacuum, so she starts singing at the top of her voice, and boy, did she have one lousy voice! We were laughing and laughing, but trying to keep it silent. Then what do you know, she stops singing and turns on the radio. And suddenly we hear Chet Baker. He's singing "I Fall in Love Too Easily", nice and slow and mellow. And Lindy and me, we just lay there across the bed together, listening to Chet singing. And after a while, I'm singing along, really soft, singing along with Chet Baker on the radio, Lindy curled up in my arms. That's how it was. That's why we're gonna do that song tonight. I don't know if she'll remember though. Who the hell knows?'

Mr Gardner stopped talking and I could see him wiping away tears. Vittorio brought us around another corner and I realised we were going past the restaurant a second time.

It looked even more lively than before, and a pianist, this guy I know called Andrea, was now playing in the corner.

As we drifted again into the dark, I said: 'Mr Gardner, it's none of my business, I know. But I can see maybe things haven't been so good between you and Mrs Gardner lately. I want you to know I understand about things like that. My mother often used to get sad, maybe just the way you are now. She'd think she'd found someone, she'd be so happy and tell me this guy was going to be my new dad. The first couple of times I believed her. After that, I knew it wouldn't work out. But my mother, she never stopped believing it. And every time she felt down, maybe like you are tonight, you know what she did? She put on your records and sang along. All those long winters, in that tiny apartment of ours, she'd sit there, knees tucked up under her, glass of something in her hand, and she'd sing along softly. And sometimes, I remember this, Mr Gardner, our neighbours upstairs would bang on the ceiling, especially when you were doing those big up-tempo numbers, like "High Hopes" or "They All Laughed". I used to watch my mother carefully, but it was like she hadn't heard a thing, she'd be listening to you, nodding her head to the beat, her lips moving with the lyrics. Mr Gardner, I wanted to say to you. Your music helped my mother through those times, it must have helped millions of others. And it's only right it should help you too.' I did a little laugh, which I meant to be encouraging, but it came out louder than I'd intended. 'You can count on me tonight, Mr Gardner. I'm going to put everything I've got into it. I'll make it as good as any orchestra, you just see. And Mrs Gardner will hear us and who knows? Maybe things will start going fine between you again. Every couple goes through difficult times.'

Mr Gardner smiled. 'You're a sweet guy. I appreciate you helping me out tonight. But we don't have any more time to talk. Lindy's in her room now. I can see the light on.'

We were going by a palazzo we'd passed at least twice before, and I now realised why Vittorio had been taking us round in circles. Mr Gardner had been watching for the light to come on in a particular window, and each time he'd found it still dark, we'd moved on to do another circle. This time, though, the third-storey window was lit, the shutters were open, and from down where we were, we could see a small part of the ceiling with its dark wooden beams. Mr Gardner signalled to Vittorio, but he'd already stopped rowing and we drifted slowly till the gondola was directly beneath the window.

Mr Gardner stood up, making the boat rock alarmingly again, and Vittorio had to move quickly to steady us. Then Mr Gardner called up, much too softly: 'Lindy? Lindy?' Finally he called out much louder: 'Lindy!'

A hand pushed the shutters out wider, then a figure came onto the narrow balcony. A lantern was fixed to the palazzo wall not far above us, but the light wasn't good, and Mrs Gardner wasn't much more than a silhouette. I could see though that she'd put up her hair since I'd met her in the piazza, maybe for their dinner earlier on.

'That you, sweetie?' She leaned over the balcony rail. 'I thought you'd been kidnapped or something. You had me all anxious.'

'Don't be foolish, honey. What could happen in a town like this? Anyway, I left you that note.'

'I didn't see any note, sweetie.'

'I left you a note. Just so you wouldn't get anxious.'

'Where is it, this note? What did it say?'

'I don't remember, honey.' Mr Gardner now sounded irritated. 'It was just a regular note. You know, saying I'd gone to buy cigarettes or something.'

'Is that what you're doing down there now? Buying cigarettes?'

'No, honey. This is something different. I'm gonna sing to you.'

'Is this some sort of joke?'

'No, honey, it isn't a joke. This is Venice. It's what people do here.' He gestured around to me and Vittorio, like our being there proved his point.

'It's kind of chilly for me out here, sweetie.'

Mr Gardner did a big sigh. 'Then you can listen from inside the room. Go back in the room, honey, make yourself comfortable. Just leave those windows open and you'll hear us fine.'

She went on gazing down at him for a while, and he went on gazing back up, neither of them saying anything. Then she'd gone inside, and Mr Gardner seemed disappointed, even though this was exactly what he'd suggested she should do. He lowered his head with another sigh, and I could tell he was hesitating about going ahead. So I said:

'Come on, Mr Gardner, let's do it. Let's do "By the Time I Get to Phoenix".'

And I played gently a little opening figure, no beat yet,

the sort of thing that could lead into a song or just as easily fade away. I tried to make it sound like America, sad roadside bars, big long highways, and I guess I was thinking too of my mother, the way I'd come into the room and see her on the sofa gazing at her record sleeve with its picture of an American road, or maybe of the singer sitting in an American car. What I mean is, I tried to play it so my mother would have recognised it as coming from that same world, the world on her record sleeve.

Then before I realised it, before I'd picked up any steady beat, Mr Gardner started to sing. His posture, standing in the gondola, was pretty unsteady, and I was afraid he'd lose his balance any moment. But his voice came out just the way I remembered it – gentle, almost husky, but with a huge amount of body, like it was coming through an invisible mike. And like all the best American singers, there was that weariness in his voice, even a hint of hesitation, like he's not a man accustomed to laying open his heart this way. That's how all the greats do it.

We went through that song, full of travelling and goodbye. An American man leaving his woman. He keeps thinking of her as he passes through the towns one by one, verse by verse, Phoenix, Albuquerque, Oklahoma, driving down a long road the way my mother never could. If only we could leave things behind like that – I guess that's what my mother would have thought. If only sadness could be like that.

We came to the end and Mr Gardner said: 'Okay, let's go straight to the next one. "I Fall in Love Too Easily".'

This being my first time playing with Mr Gardner, I

had to feel my way around everything, but we managed okay. After what he'd told me about this song, I kept looking up at that window, but there was nothing from Mrs Gardner, no movement, no sound, nothing. Then we'd finished, and the quiet and the dark settled around us. Somewhere nearby, I could hear a neighbour pushing open shutters, maybe to hear better. But nothing from Mrs Gardner's window.

We did 'One for My Baby' very slow, virtually no beat at all, then everything was silent again. We went on looking up at the window, then at last, maybe after a full minute, we heard it. You could only just make it out, but there was no mistaking it. Mrs Gardner was up there sobbing.

'We did it, Mr Gardner!' I whispered. 'We did it. We got her by the heart.'

But Mr Gardner didn't seem pleased. He shook his head tiredly, sat down and gestured to Vittorio. 'Take us round the other side. It's time I went in.'

As we started to move again, I thought he was avoiding looking at me, almost like he was ashamed of what we'd just done, and I began thinking maybe this whole plan had been some kind of malicious joke. For all I knew, these songs all held horrible meanings for Mrs Gardner. So I put my guitar away and sat there, maybe a bit sullen, and that's how we travelled for a while.

Then we came out to a much wider canal, and immediately a water-taxi coming the other way rushed past us, making waves under the gondola. But we were nearly up to the front of Mr Gardner's palazzo, and as Vittorio let us drift towards the quay, I said:

'Mr Gardner, you've been an important part of my growing up. And tonight's been a very special night for me. If we just said goodbye now and I never saw you again, I know for the rest of my life I'll always be wondering. So Mr Gardner, please tell me. Just now, was Mrs Gardner crying because she was happy or because she was upset?'

I thought he wasn't going to answer. In the dim light, his figure was just this hunched-up shape at the front of the boat. But as Vittorio was tying the rope, he said quietly:

'I guess she was pleased to hear me sing that way. But sure, she was upset. We're both of us upset. Twenty-seven years is a long time and after this trip we're separating. This is our last trip together.'

'I'm really sorry to hear that, Mr Gardner,' I said gently. 'I guess a lot of marriages come to an end, even after twenty-seven years. But at least you're able to part like this. A holiday in Venice. Singing from a gondola. There can't be many couples who split up and stay so civilised.'

'But why wouldn't we be civilised? We still love each other. That's why she's crying up there. Because she still loves me as much as I still love her.'

Vittorio had stepped up onto the quay, but Mr Gardner and I kept sitting in the darkness. I was waiting for him to say more, and sure enough, after a moment, he went on:

'Like I told you, the first time I laid eyes on Lindy I fell in love with her. But did she love me back then? I doubt if the question ever crossed her mind. I was a star, that's all that mattered to her. I was what she'd dreamt of, what she'd planned to win for herself back in that little diner.

Whether she loved me or not didn't come into it. But twenty-seven years of marriage can do funny things. Plenty of couples, they start off loving each other, then get tired of each other, end up hating each other. Sometimes though it goes the other way. It took a few years, but bit by bit, Lindy began to love me. I didn't dare believe it at first, but after a while there was nothing else to believe. A little touch on my shoulder as we were getting up from a table. A funny little smile across the room when there wasn't anything to smile about, just her fooling around. I bet she was as surprised as anyone, but that's what happened. After five or six years, we found we were easy with each other. That we worried about each other, cared about each other. Like I say, we loved each other. And we still love each other today.'

'I don't get it, Mr Gardner. So why are you and Mrs Gardner separating?'

He did another of his sighs. 'How would you understand, my friend, coming from where you do? But you've been kind to me tonight, so I'm gonna try and explain it. Fact is, I'm no longer the major name I once was. Protest all you like, but where we come from, there's no getting round something like that. I'm no longer a major name. Now I could just accept that and fade away. Live on past glories. Or I could say, no, I'm not finished yet. In other words, my friend, I could make a comeback. Plenty have from my position and worse. But a comeback's no easy game. You have to be prepared to make a lot of changes, some of them hard ones. You change the way you are. You even change some things you love.'

'Mr Gardner, are you saying you and Mrs Gardner have to separate because of your comeback?'

'Look at the other guys, the guys who came back successfully. Look at the ones from my generation still hanging round. Every single one of them, they've remarried. Twice, sometimes three times. Every one of them, young wives on their arms. Me and Lindy are getting to be a laughing stock. Besides, there's been this particular young lady I've had my eye on, and she's had her eye on me. Lindy knows the score. She's known it longer than I have, maybe ever since those days in that diner listening to Meg. We've talked it over. She understands it's time to go our separate ways.'

'I still don't get it, Mr Gardner. This place you and Mrs Gardner come from can't be so different from everywhere else. That's why, Mr Gardner, that's why these songs you've been singing all these years, they make sense for people everywhere. Even where I used to live. And what do all these songs say? If two people fall out of love and they have to part, then that's sad. But if they go on loving each other, they should stay together for ever. That's what these songs are saying.'

'I understand what you're saying, friend. And it might sound hard to you, I know. But that's the way it is. And listen, this is about Lindy too. It's best for her we do this now. She's nowhere near old yet. You've seen her, she's still a beautiful woman. She needs to get out now, while she has time. Time to find love again, make another marriage. She needs to get out before it's too late.'

I don't know what I would have said to that, but then he

caught me by surprise, saying: 'Your mother. I guess she never got out.'

I thought about it, then said quietly: 'No, Mr Gardner. She never got out. She didn't live long enough to see the changes in our country.'

'That's too bad. I'm sure she was a fine woman. If what you say is true, and my music helped make her happy, that means a lot to me. Too bad she didn't get out. I don't want that to happen to my Lindy. No, sir. Not to my Lindy. I want my Lindy to get out.'

The gondola was bumping gently against the quay. Vittorio called out softly, reaching out his hand, and after a few seconds, Mr Gardner got to his feet and climbed out. By the time I too had climbed out with my guitar – I wasn't going to beg any free rides from Vittorio – Mr Gardner had his wallet out.

Vittorio seemed pleased with what he was given, and with his usual fine phrases and gestures, he got back in his gondola and set off down the canal.

We watched him disappear into the dark, then next thing, Mr Gardner was pushing a lot of notes into my hand. I told him it was way too much, that anyway it was a huge honour for me, but he wouldn't hear of taking any of it back.

'No, no,' he said, waving his hand in front of his face, like he wanted to be done, not just with the money, but with me, the evening, maybe this whole section of his life. He started to walk off towards his palazzo, but after a few paces, he stopped and turned back to look at me. The little street we were in, the canal, everything was silent now except for the distant sound of a television.

'You played well tonight, my friend,' he said. 'You have a nice touch.'

'Thank you, Mr Gardner. And you sang great. As great as ever.'

'Maybe I'll come by the square again before we leave. Listen to you playing with your crew.'

'I hope so, Mr Gardner.'

But I never saw him again. I heard a few months later, in the autumn, that Mr and Mrs Gardner got their divorce – one of the waiters at the Florian read it somewhere and told me. It all came back to me then about that evening, and it made me feel a little sad thinking about it again. Because Mr Gardner had seemed a pretty decent guy, and whichever way you look at it, comeback or no comeback, he'll always be one of the greats.

Come Rain or Come Shine

Like me, Emily loved old American Broadway songs. She'd go more for the up-tempo numbers, like Irving Berlin's 'Cheek to Cheek' and Cole Porter's 'Begin the Beguine', while I'd lean towards the bitter-sweet ballads – 'Here's That Rainy Day' or 'It Never Entered My Mind'. But there was a big overlap, and anyway, back then, on a university campus in the south of England, it was a near-miracle to find anyone else who shared such passions. Today, a young person's likely to listen to any sort of music. My nephew, who starts university this autumn, is going through his Argentinian tango phase. He also likes Edith Piaf as well as any number of the latest indie bands. But in our day tastes weren't nearly so diverse. My fellow students fell into two broad camps: the hippie types with their long hair and flowing garments who liked 'progressive rock', and the neat, tweedy ones who considered anything other than classical music a horrible din. Occasionally you'd bump into someone who professed to be into jazz, but this would always turn out to be of the so-called crossover kind – endless improvisations with no respect for the beautifully crafted songs used as their starting points.

So it was a relief to discover someone else, and a girl at

that, who appreciated the Great American Songbook. Like me, Emily collected LPs with sensitive, straightforward vocal interpretations of the standards – you could often find such records going cheap in junk shops, discarded by our parents' generation. She favoured Sarah Vaughan and Chet Baker. I preferred Julie London and Peggy Lee. Neither of us was big on Sinatra or Ella Fitzgerald.

In that first year, Emily lived in college, and she had in her room a portable record player, a type that was quite common then. It looked like a large hat box, with pale-blue leatherette surfaces and a single built-in speaker. Only when you raised its lid would you see the turntable sitting inside. It gave out a pretty primitive sound by today's standards, but I remember us crouching around it happily for hours, taking off one track, carefully lowering the needle down onto another. We loved playing different versions of the same song, then arguing about the lyrics, or about the singers' interpretations. Was that line really supposed to be sung so ironically? Was it better to sing 'Georgia on My Mind' as though Georgia was a woman or the place in America? We were especially pleased when we found a recording – like Ray Charles singing 'Come Rain or Come Shine' – where the words themselves were happy, but the interpretation was pure heartbreak.

Emily's love of these records was obviously so deep that I'd be taken aback each time I stumbled on her talking to other students about some pretentious rock band or vacuous Californian singer-songwriter. At times, she'd start arguing about a 'concept' album in much the way she and I would discuss Gershwin or Howard Arlen, and then I'd have to bite my lip not to show my irritation.

Back then, Emily was slim and beautiful, and if she hadn't settled on Charlie so early in her university career, I'm sure she'd have had a whole bunch of men competing for her. But she was never flirty or tarty, so once she was with Charlie, the other suitors backed off.

'That's the only reason I keep Charlie around,' she told me once, with a dead straight face, then burst out laughing when I looked shocked. 'Just a joke, silly. Charlie is my darling, my darling, my darling.'

Charlie was my best friend at university. During that first year, we hung around together the whole time and that was how I'd come to know Emily. In the second year, Charlie and Emily got a house-share down in town, and though I was a frequent visitor, those discussions with Emily around her record-player became a thing of the past. For a start, whenever I called round to the house, there were several other students sitting around, laughing and talking, and there was now a fancy stereo system churning out rock music you had to shout over.

Charlie and I have remained close friends through the years. We may not see each other as much as we once did, but that's mainly down to distances. I've spent years here in Spain, as well as in Italy and Portugal, while Charlie's always based himself in London. Now if that makes it sound like I'm the jet-setter and he's the stay-at-home, that would be funny. Because in fact Charlie's the one who's always flying off – to Texas, Tokyo, New York – to his high-powered meetings, while I've been stuck in the same humid buildings year after year, setting spelling tests or conducting the same conversations in slowed-down English. My-name-is-Ray. What-is-your-name? Do-you-have-children?

When I first took up English teaching after university, it seemed a good enough life – much like an extension of university. Language schools were mushrooming all over Europe, and if the teaching was tedious and the hours exploitative, at that age you don't care too much. You spend a lot of time in bars, friends are easy to make, and there's a feeling you're part of a large network extending around the entire globe. You meet people fresh from their spells in Peru or Thailand, and this gets you thinking that if you wanted to, you could drift around the world indefinitely, using your contacts to get a job in any faraway corner you fancied. And always you'd be part of this cosy, extended family of itinerant teachers, swapping stories over drinks about former colleagues, psychotic school directors, eccentric British Council officers.

In the late '80s, there was talk of making a lot of money teaching in Japan, and I made serious plans to go, but it never worked out. I thought about Brazil too, even read a few books about the culture and sent off for application forms. But somehow I never got away that far. Southern Italy, Portugal for a short spell, back here to Spain. Then before you know it, you're forty-seven years old, and the people you started out with have long ago been replaced by a generation who gossip about different things, take different drugs and listen to different music.

Meanwhile, Charlie and Emily had married and settled down in London. Charlie told me once, when they had children I'd be godfather to one of them. But that never happened. What I mean is, a child never came along, and now I suppose it's too late. I have to admit, I've always felt slightly let down about this. Perhaps I always imagined that being godfather to one of their children would provide an official link, however tenuous, between their lives in England and mine out here.

Anyway, at the start of this summer, I went to London to stay with them. It had been arranged well in advance, and when I'd phoned to check a couple of days beforehand, Charlie had said they were both 'superbly well'. That's why I'd no reason to expect anything other than pampering and relaxation after a few months that hadn't exactly been the best in my life.

In fact, as I emerged out of their local Underground that sunny day, my thoughts were on the possible refinements that might have been added to 'my' bedroom since the previous visit. Over the years, there's almost always been something or other. One time it was some gleaming electronic gadget standing in the corner; another time the whole place had been redecorated. In any case, almost as a point of principle, the room would be prepared for me the way a posh hotel would go about things: towels laid out, a bedside tin of biscuits, a selection of CDs on the dressing table. A few years ago, Charlie had led me in and with nonchalant pride started flicking switches, causing all sorts of subtly hidden lights to go on and off: behind the headboard, above the wardrobe and so on. Another switch had triggered a growling hum and blinds had begun to descend over the two windows.

'Look, Charlie, why do I need blinds?' I'd asked that time. 'I want to see out when I wake up. Just the curtains will do fine.'

'These blinds are Swiss,' he'd said, as though this were explanation enough.

But this time Charlie led me up the stairs mumbling to himself, and as we got to my room, I realised he was making excuses. And then I saw the room as I'd never seen it before. The bed was bare, the mattress on it mottled and askew. On the floor were piles of magazines and paper-backs, bundles of old clothes, a hockey stick and a loudspeaker fallen on its side. I paused at the threshold and stared at it while Charlie cleared a space to put down my bag.

'You look like you're about to demand to see the man-ager,' he said, bitterly.

'No, no. It's just that it's unusual to see it this way.'

'It's a mess, I know. A mess.' He sat down on the mat-tress and sighed. 'I thought the cleaning girls would have sorted all this. But of course they haven't. God knows why not.'

He seemed very dejected, but then he suddenly sprang to his feet again.

'Look, let's go out for some lunch. I'll leave a note for Emily. We can have a long leisurely lunch and by the time we come back, your room – the whole flat – will be sorted out.'

'But we can't ask Emily to tidy everything.'

'Oh, she won't do it herself. She'll get on to the cleaners. She knows how to harass them. Me, I don't even have their number. Lunch, let's have lunch. Three courses, bottle of wine, everything.'

What Charlie called their flat was in fact the top two floors of a four-storey terrace in a well-to-do but busy street. We came out of the front door straight into a throng of people and traffic. I followed Charlie past shops and offices to a smart little Italian restaurant. We didn't have a reservation, but the waiters greeted Charlie like a friend and led us to a table. Looking around I saw the place was full of business types in suits and ties, and I was glad Charlie looked as scruffy as I did. He must have guessed my thoughts, because as we sat down he said:

'Oh, you're so home counties, Ray. Anyway, it's all changed now. You've been out of the country too long.' Then in an alarmingly loud voice: '*We* look like the ones who've made it. Everyone else here looks like middle management.' Then he leant towards me and said more quietly: 'Look, we've got to talk. I need you to do me a favour.'

I couldn't remember the last time Charlie had asked my help for anything, but I managed a casual nod and waited. He played with his menu for a few seconds, then put it down.

'The truth is, Emily and I have been going through a bit of a sticky patch. In fact, just recently, we've been avoiding one another altogether. That's why she wasn't there just now to welcome you. Right now, I'm afraid, you get a choice of one or the other of us. A bit like those plays when the same actor's playing two parts. You can't get both me and Emily in the same room at the same time. Rather childish, isn't it?'

[43]

'This is obviously a bad time for me to have come. I'll go away, straight after lunch. I'll stay with my Auntie Katie in Finchley.'

'What are you talking about? You're not listening. I just told you. I want you to do me a favour.'

'I thought that was your way of saying . . .'

'No, you idiot, *I'm* the one who has to clear out. I've got to go to a meeting in Frankfurt, I'm flying out this afternoon. I'll be back in two days, Thursday at the latest. Meanwhile, you stay here. You bring things round, make everything okay again. Then I come back, say a cheerful hello, kiss my darling wife like the last two months haven't happened, and we pick up again.'

At this point the waitress came to take our order, and after she'd gone Charlie seemed reluctant to take up the subject again. Instead, he fired questions at me about my life in Spain, and each time I told him anything, good or bad, he'd do this sour little smile and shake his head, like I was confirming his worst fears. At one point I was trying to tell him how much I'd improved as a cook – how I'd prepared the Christmas buffet for over forty students and teachers virtually single-handed – but he just cut me off in mid-sentence.

'Listen to me,' he said. 'Your situation's hopeless. You've got to hand in your notice. But first, you have to get your new job lined up. This Portuguese depressive, use him as a go-between. Secure the Madrid post, then ditch the apartment. Okay, here's what you do. One.'

He held up his hand and began counting off each instruction as he made it. Our food arrived when he still had a couple of fingers to go, but he ignored it and carried on till he'd finished. Then as we began to eat, he said:

'I can tell you won't do any of this.'

'No, no, everything you say is very sound.'

'You'll go back and carry on just the same. Then we'll be here again in a year's time and you'll be moaning about exactly the same things.'

'I wasn't moaning . . .'

'You know, Ray, there's only so much other people can suggest to you. After a certain point, you've got to take charge of your life.'

'Okay, I will, I promise. But you were saying earlier, something about a favour.'

'Ah yes.' He chewed his food thoughtfully. 'To be honest, this was my real motive in inviting you over. Of course, it's great to see you and all of that. But for me, the main thing, I wanted you to do something for me. After all you're my oldest friend, a life-long friend . . .'

Suddenly he began eating again, and I realised with astonishment he was sobbing quietly. I reached across the table and prodded his shoulder, but he just kept shovelling pasta into his mouth without looking up. When this had gone on for a minute or so, I reached over and gave him another little prod, but this had no more effect than my first one. Then the waitress appeared with a cheerful smile to check on our food. We both said everything was excellent and as she went off, Charlie seemed to become more himself again.

'Okay, Ray, listen. What I'm asking you to do is dead simple. All I want is for you to hang about with Emily for the next few days, be a pleasant guest. That's all. Just until I get back.'

'That's all? You're just asking me to look after her while you're gone?'

'That's it. Or rather, let her look after you. You're the guest. I've lined up some things for you to do. Theatre tickets and so on. I'll be back Thursday at the latest. Your mission's just to get her in a good mood and keep her that way. So when I come in and say, "Hello darling," and hug her, she'll just reply, "Oh hello, darling, welcome home, how was everything," and hug me back. Then we can carry on as before. Before all this horrible stuff began. That's your mission. Quite simple really.'

'I'm happy to do anything I can,' I said. 'But look, Charlie, are you sure she's in the mood to entertain visitors? You're obviously going through some sort of crisis. She must be as upset as you are. Quite honestly, I don't understand why you asked me here right now.'

'What do you mean, you don't understand? I've asked you because you're my oldest friend. Yes, all right, I've got a lot of friends. But when it comes down to it, when I thought hard about it, I realised you're the only one who'd do.'

I have to admit I was rather moved by this. All the same, I could see there was something not quite right here, something he wasn't telling me.

'I can understand you inviting me to stay if you were both going to be here,' I said. 'I can see how that would work. You're not talking to each other, you invite a guest as a diversion, you both put on your best behaviour, things start to thaw. But it's not going to work in this case, because you're not going to be here.'

'Just do it for me, Ray. I think it might work. Emily's always cheered up by you.'

'Cheered up by me? You know, Charlie, I want to help. But it's possible you've got this a bit wrong. Because I get the impression, quite frankly, Emily isn't cheered up by me at all, even at the best of times. The last few visits here, she was . . . well, distinctly impatient with me.'

'Look, Ray, just trust me. I know what I'm doing.'

Emily was at the flat when we returned. I have to admit, I was taken aback at how much she'd aged. It wasn't just that she'd got significantly heavier since my last visit: her face, once so effortlessly graceful, was now distinctly bull-doggy, with a displeased set to the mouth. She was sitting on the living-room sofa reading the *Financial Times*, and got up rather glumly as I came in.

'Nice to see you, Raymond,' she said, kissing me quickly on the cheek, then sitting down again. The whole way she did this made me want to blurt out a profuse apology for intruding at such a bad time. But before I could say anything, she thumped the space beside her on the sofa, saying: 'Now, Raymond, sit down here and answer my questions. I want to know all about what you've been up to.'

I sat down and she began to interrogate me, much as Charlie had done in the restaurant. Charlie, meanwhile, was packing for his journey, drifting in and out of the room in search of various items. I noticed they didn't look at each

other, but neither did they seem so uncomfortable being in
the same room, despite what he'd claimed. And although
they never spoke directly to each other, Charlie kept join-
ing in the conversation in an odd, once-removed manner.
For instance, when I was explaining to Emily why it was so
difficult to find a flat-mate to share my rent burden,
Charlie shouted from the kitchen:

'The place he's in, it's just not geared up for two people!
It's for one person, and one person with a bit more money
than he'll ever have!'

Emily made no response to this, but must have absorbed
the information, because she then went on: 'Raymond, you
should never have chosen an apartment like that.'

This sort of thing continued for at least the next twenty
minutes, Charlie making his contributions from the stairs
or as he passed through to the kitchen, usually by shouting
out some statement that referred to me in the third person.
At one point, Emily suddenly said:

'Oh, honestly Raymond. You let yourself be exploited
left, right and centre by that ghastly language school, you
let your landlord rip you off silly, and what do you do? Get
in tow with some airhead girl with a drink problem and
not even a job to support it. It's like you're deliberately trying to annoy anyone who still gives a shit about you!'

'He can't expect many of that tribe to survive!' Charlie
boomed from the hall. I could hear he had his suitcase out
there now. 'It's all very well behaving like an adolescent ten
years after you've ceased to be one. But to carry on like this
when you're nearly fifty!'

'I'm only forty-seven . . .'

[48]

'What do you mean, you're *only* forty-seven?' Emily's voice was unnecessarily loud given I was sitting right next to her. '*Only* forty-seven. This "only", this is what's destroying your life, Raymond. Only, only, only. Only doing my best. Only forty-seven. Soon you'll be only *sixty*-seven and only going round in bloody circles trying to find a bloody roof to keep over your head!'

'He needs to get his bloody arse together!' Charlie yelled down the staircase. 'Fucking well pull his socks up till they're touching his fucking balls!'

'Raymond, don't you ever stop and ask yourself who you are?' Emily asked. 'When you think of all your potential, aren't you ashamed? Look at how you lead your life! It's . . . it's simply infuriating! One gets so exasperated!'

Charlie appeared in the doorway in his raincoat, and for a moment they were shouting different things at me simultaneously. Then Charlie broke off, announced he was leaving – as though in disgust at me – and vanished.

His departure brought Emily's diatribe to a halt, and I took the opportunity to get to my feet, saying: 'Excuse me, I'll just go and give Charlie a hand with his luggage.'

'Why do I need help with my luggage?' Charlie said from the hall. 'I've only got the one bag.'

But he let me follow him down into the street and left me with the suitcase while he went to the edge of the kerb to hail a cab. There didn't seem to be any to hand, and he leaned out worriedly, an arm half-raised.

I went up to him and said: 'Charlie, I don't think it's going to work.'

'What's not going to work?'

'Emily absolutely hates me. That's her after seeing me for a few minutes. What's she going to be like after three days? Why on earth do you think you'll come back to harmony and light?'

Even as I was saying this, something was dawning on me and I fell silent. Noticing the change, Charlie turned and looked at me carefully.

'I think', I said, eventually, 'I have an idea why it had to be me and no one else.'

'Ah ha. Can it be Ray sees the light?'

'Yes, maybe I do.'

'But what does it matter? It remains the same, exactly the same, what I'm asking you to do.' Now there were tears in his eyes again. 'Do you remember, Ray, the way Emily always used to say she believed in me? She said it for years and years. I believe in you, Charlie, you can go all the way, you're really talented. Right up until three, four years ago, she was still saying it. Do you know how trying that got? I was doing all right. I *am* doing all right. Perfectly okay. But she thought I was destined for . . . God knows, president of the fucking world, God knows! I'm just an ordinary bloke who's doing all right. But she doesn't see that. That's at the heart of it, at the heart of everything that's gone wrong.'

He began to walk slowly along the pavement, very preoccupied. I hurried back to get his suitcase and began pulling it along on its rollers. The street was still fairly crowded, so it was a struggle to keep up with him without crashing the bag into other pedestrians. But Charlie kept walking at a steady pace, oblivious to my difficulties.

'She thinks I've let myself down,' he was saying. 'But I haven't. I'm doing perfectly okay. Endless horizons are all very well when you're young. But get to our age, you've got to . . . you've got to get some perspective. That's what kept going round in my head whenever she got unbearable about it. Perspective, she needs perspective. And I kept saying to myself, look, I'm doing okay. Look at loads of other people, people we know. Look at Ray. Look what a pig's arse he's making of *his* life. She needs perspective.'

'So you decided to invite me for a visit. To be Mr Perspective.'

At last, Charlie stopped and met my eye. 'Don't get me wrong, Ray. I'm not saying you're an awful failure or anything. I realise you're not a drug addict or a murderer. But beside me, let's face it, you don't look the highest of achievers. That's why I'm asking you, asking you to do this for me. Things are on their last legs with us, I'm desperate, I need you to help. And what am I asking, for God's sake? Just that you be your usual sweet self. Nothing more, nothing less. Just do it for me, Raymond. For me and Emily. It's not over between us yet, I know it isn't. Just be yourself for a few days until I get back. That's not so much to ask, is it?'

I took a deep breath and said: 'Okay, okay, if you think it'll help. But isn't Emily going to see through all this sooner or later?'

'Why should she? She knows I've got an important meeting in Frankfurt. To her the whole thing's straightforward. She's just looking after a guest, that's all. She likes to do that and she likes you. Look, a taxi.' He waved frantically and as the driver came towards us, he grasped my arm. 'Thanks, Ray. You'll swing it for us, I know you will.'

I returned to find Emily's manner had undergone a complete transformation. She welcomed me into the apartment the way she might a very aged and frail relative. There were encouraging smiles, gentle touches on the arm. When I agreed to some tea, she led me into the kitchen, sat me down at the table, then for a few seconds stood there regarding me with a concerned expression. Eventually she said, softly:

'I'm so sorry I went on at you like that earlier, Raymond. I've got no right to talk to you like that.' Then turning away to make the tea, she went on: 'It's years now since we were at university together. I always forget that. I'd never dream of talking to any other friend that way. But when it's you, well, I suppose I look at you and it's like we're back there, the way we all were then, and I just forget. You really mustn't take it to heart.'

'No, no. I haven't taken it to heart at all.' I was still thinking about the conversation I'd just had with Charlie, and probably seemed distant. I think Emily misinterpreted this, because her voice became even more gentle.

'I'm so sorry I upset you.' She was carefully laying out rows of biscuits on a plate in front of me. 'The thing is, Raymond, back in those days, we could say virtually anything to you, you'd just laugh and we'd laugh, and everything would be a big joke. It's so silly of me, thinking you could still be like that.'

'Well, actually, I *am* more or less still like that. I didn't think anything of it.'

'I didn't realise', she went on, apparently not hearing me, 'how different you are now. How close to the edge you must be.'

'Look, really Emily, I'm not so bad . . .'

'I suppose the passing years have just left you high and dry. You're like a man on the precipice. One more tiny push and you'll crack.'

'Fall, you mean.'

She'd been fiddling with the kettle, but now turned round to stare at me again. 'No, Raymond, don't talk like that. Not even in fun. I don't ever want to hear you talking like that.'

'No, you misunderstand. You said I'd crack, but if I'm on a precipice, then I'd fall, not crack.'

'Oh, you poor thing.' She still didn't seem to take in what I was saying. 'You're only a husk of the Raymond from those days.'

I decided it might be best not to respond this time, and for a few moments we waited quietly for the kettle to boil. She prepared a cup for me, though not for herself, and placed it in front of me.

'I'm so sorry, Ray, but I've got to get back to the office now. There are two meetings I absolutely can't miss. If only I'd known how you'd be, I wouldn't have deserted you. I'd have made other arrangements. But I haven't, I'm expected back. Poor Raymond. What will you do here, all by yourself?'

'I'll be terrific. Really. In fact, I was thinking. Why don't I get our dinner ready while you're gone? You probably won't believe this, but I've become a pretty good cook these days. In fact, we had this buffet just before Christmas . . .'

'That's terribly sweet of you, wanting to help. But I think it's best you rest just now. After all, an unfamiliar kitchen can be the source of so much stress. Why don't you just make yourself completely at home, have a herbal bath, listen to some music. I'll take care of dinner when I come in.'

'But you don't want to worry about food after a long day at the office.'

'No, Ray, you're just to relax.' She produced a business card and placed it on the table. 'This has got my direct line on it, my mobile too. I've *got* to go now, but you can call me any time you want. Now remember, don't take on anything stressful while I'm gone.'

For some time now I've been finding it hard to relax properly in my own apartment. If I'm alone at home, I get increasingly restless, bothered by the idea that I'm missing some crucial encounter out there somewhere. But if I'm left by myself in someone else's place, I often find a nice sense of peace engulfing me. I love sinking into an unfamiliar sofa with whatever book happens to be lying nearby. And that's exactly what I did this time, after Emily had left. Or at least, I managed to read a couple of chapters of *Mansfield Park* before dozing off for twenty minutes or so.

When I woke up, the afternoon sun was coming into the flat. Getting off the sofa, I began a little nose-around. Perhaps the cleaners had indeed been in during our lunch, or maybe Emily had done the tidying herself; in any case, the large living room was looking pretty immaculate. Tidiness aside, it had been stylishly done up, with modern designer furniture and arty objects – though someone being unkind might have said it was all too obviously for effect. I took a browse through the books, then glanced through the CD collection. It was almost entirely rock or classical, but finally, after some searching, I found tucked away in the shadows a small section devoted to Fred Astaire, Chet Baker, Sarah Vaughan. It puzzled me that Emily hadn't replaced more of her treasured vinyl collection with their CD reincarnations, but I didn't dwell on this, and wandered off into the kitchen.

I was opening up a few cupboards in search of biscuits or a chocolate bar when I noticed what seemed to be a small notebook on the kitchen table. It had purple cushioned covers, which made it stand out amidst the sleek minimalist surfaces of the kitchen. Emily, in a big hurry just before she'd left, had been emptying and re-filling her bag on the table while I'd been drinking my tea. Obviously she'd left the notebook behind by mistake. But then in almost the next instant another idea came to me: that this purple book was some kind of intimate diary, and Emily had left it there on purpose, fully intending for me to have a peek; that for whatever reason, she'd felt unable to confide more openly, so had resorted to this way of sharing her inner turmoil.

I stood there for a while, staring at the notebook. Then I reached forward, inserted my forefinger into the pages at the mid-way point and gingerly levered it up. The sight of Emily's closely packed handwriting inside made me pull my finger out, and I moved away from the table, telling myself I had no business nosing in there, never mind what Emily had intended in an irrational moment.

I went back into the living room, settled into the sofa and read a few more pages of *Mansfield Park*. But now I found I couldn't concentrate. My mind kept going back to the purple notebook. What if it hadn't been an impulsive action at all? What if she'd planned this for days? What if she'd composed something carefully for me to read?

After another ten minutes, I went back into the kitchen and stared some more at the purple notebook. Then I sat down, where I'd sat before to drink my tea, slid the note-book towards me, and opened it.

One thing that became quickly apparent was that if Emily confided her innermost thoughts to a diary, then that book was elsewhere. What I had before me was at best a glorified appointments diary; under each day she'd scrawled various memos to herself, some with a distinct aspirational dimension. One entry in bold felt-tip went: 'If still not phoned Mathilda, WHY THE HELL NOT??? DO IT!!!'

Another one ran: 'Finish Philip Bloody Roth. Give back to Marion!'

Then, as I kept turning the pages, I came across: 'Raymond coming Monday. Groan, groan.'

I turned a couple more pages to find: 'Ray tomorrow. How to survive?'

Finally, written that very morning, amidst reminders for various chores: 'Buy wine for arrival of Prince of Whiners.'

Prince of Whiners? It took me some time to accept this really could be referring to me. I tried out all sorts of possibilities – a client? a plumber? – but in the end, given the date and the context, I had to accept there was no other serious candidate. Then suddenly the sheer unfairness of her giving me such a title hit me with unexpected force, and before I knew it, I'd screwed up the offending page in my hand.

It wasn't a particularly fierce action: I didn't even tear the page. I'd simply closed my fist on it in a single motion, and the next second I was in control again, but of course, by then, it was too late. I opened my hand to discover not only the page in question but also the two beneath it had fallen victim to my wrath. I tried to flatten the pages back to their original form, but they simply curled back up again, as though their deepest wish was to be transformed into a ball of rubbish.

All the same, for quite some time, I carried on performing a kind of panicked ironing motion on the damaged pages. I was just about coming to accept that my efforts were pointless – that nothing I now did could successfully conceal what I'd done – when I became aware of a phone ringing somewhere in the apartment.

I decided to ignore it, and went on trying to think through the implications of what had just happened. But then the answering machine came on and I could hear Charlie's voice leaving a message. Perhaps I sensed a lifeline, perhaps I just wanted someone to confide in, but I found myself rushing into the living room and grabbing the phone off the glass coffee table.

'Oh, you *are* there.' Charlie sounded slightly cross I'd interrupted his message.

'Charlie, listen. I've just done something rather stupid.'

'I'm at the airport,' he said. 'The flight's been delayed. I want to call the car service that's picking me up in Frankfurt, but I didn't bring their number. So I need you to read it over to me.'

He began to issue instructions about where I'd find the phone book, but I interrupted him, saying:

'Look, I've just done something stupid. I don't know what to do.'

There was quiet for a few seconds. Then he said: 'Maybe you're thinking, Ray. Maybe you're thinking there's someone else. That I'm going off now to see her. It occurred to me that might be what you were thinking. After all, it would fit with everything you've observed. The way Emily was when I left, all of that. But you're wrong.'

'Yes, I take your point. But look, there's something I have to talk to you about . . .'

'Just accept it, Ray. You're wrong. There's no other woman. I'm going now to Frankfurt to attend a meeting about changing our agency in Poland. That's where I'm going right now.'

'Right, I've got you.'

'There's never been another woman in any of this. I wouldn't look at anyone else, at least not in any serious way. That's the truth. It's the bloody truth and there's nothing else to it!'

He'd started to shout, though possibly this was because of all the noise around him in the departure lounge. Now he went quiet, and I listened hard to work out if he was crying again, but all I heard were airport noises. Suddenly he said:

'I know what you're thinking. You're thinking, all right, there's no other woman. But is there another *man*? Go on, admit it, that's what you're thinking, isn't it? Go on, say it!'

'Actually, no. It's never occurred to me you might be gay. Even that time after finals when you got really drunk and pretended to . . .'

'Shut up, you fool! I meant another man, as in Lover of Emily! Lover of Emily, does this figure bloody exist? That's what I'm getting at. And the answer, in my judgement, is no, no, no. After all these years, I can read her pretty well. But the trouble is, precisely because I know her so well, I can tell something else too. I can tell she's started to think about it. That's right, Ray, she's looking at other guys. Guys like David bloody Corey!'

'Who's that?'

'David bloody Corey is a smarmy git of a barrister who's doing well for himself. I know exactly how well, because she tells me how well, in excruciating detail.'

'You think . . . they're seeing each other?'

'No, I just told you! There's nothing, not yet! Anyway, David bloody Corey wouldn't give her the time of day. He's married to a glamourpuss who works for Condé Nast.'

'Then you're okay . . .'

'I'm not okay, because there's also Michael Addison. And Roger Van Den Berg who's a rising star at Merrill Lynch who gets to go to the World Economic Forum every year . . .'

'Look, Charlie, please listen. I've got this problem here. Small by most standards, I admit. But a problem all the same. Please just listen.'

At last I got to tell him what had happened. I recounted everything as honestly as I could, though maybe I went easy on the bit about my thinking Emily had left a confidential message for me.

'I know it was really stupid,' I said, as I came to the end. 'But she'd left it sitting there, right there on the kitchen table.'

'Yes.' Charlie was now sounding much calmer. 'Yes. You've rather let yourself in for it there.'

Then he laughed. Encouraged by this, I laughed too.

'I suppose I'm over-reacting,' I said. 'After all, it's not like her personal diary or anything. It's just a memo book . . .' I trailed off because Charlie had continued to laugh, and there was something a touch hysterical in his laughter. Then he stopped and said flatly:

'If she finds out, she'll want to saw your balls off.'

There was a short pause while I listened to airport noises. Then he went on:

'About six years ago, I opened that book myself, or that year's equivalent. Just casually, when I was sitting in the kitchen, and she was doing some cooking. You know, just flicked it open absent-mindedly while I was saying something. She noticed immediately and told me she wasn't happy about it. In fact, that's when she told me she would saw my balls off. She was wielding this rolling pin at the time, so I pointed out she couldn't very well do what she was threatening with a rolling pin. That's when she said the rolling pin was for afterwards. For what she'd do to them once she'd cut them off.'

A flight announcement went off in the background.

'So what do you suggest I do?' I asked.

'What *can* you do? Just keep smoothing the pages down. Maybe she won't notice.'

'I've been trying that and it just doesn't work. There's no way she won't notice . . .'

'Look, Ray, I've got a lot on my mind. What I'm trying to tell you is that all these men Emily dreams about, they're not really potential lovers. They're just figures she thinks are wonderful because she believes they've accomplished so much. She doesn't see their warts. Their sheer . . . *brutality*. They're all out of her league anyway. The point is, and this is what's so pathetically sad and ironic about all this, the point is, at the bottom of it all, she loves *me*. She still loves me. I can tell, I can tell.'

'So, Charlie, you don't have any advice.'

'No! I don't have any fucking advice!' He was shouting full blast again. 'You figure it out! You get on your plane and I'll get on mine. And we'll see which one crashes!'

With that, Charlie was gone. I slumped down into the sofa and took a deep breath. I told myself I had to keep things in proportion, but all the while I could feel in my stomach a vaguely nauseous sensation of panic. Various ideas ran through my mind. One solution was simply to flee the apartment, and have no contact with Charlie and Emily for several years, after which I'd send them a cautious, carefully worded letter. Even in my current state, I dismissed this plan as being a touch too desperate. A better plan was that I steadily work through the bottles in their drinks cabinet, so that when Emily arrived home, she'd find me pathetically drunk. Then I could claim to have looked through her diary and attacked the pages in an alcoholic delirium. In fact, in my drunken unreasonableness, I could even adopt the role of the injured party, shouting and pointing, telling her how bitterly hurt I'd been to read those words about me, written by someone whose love and friendship I'd always counted on, the thought of which had helped sustain me through my lousiest moments in strange and lonely countries. But while this plan had points to recommend it from a practical aspect, I could sense something there – something near the bottom of it, something I didn't care to examine too closely – that I knew would make it an impossibility for me.

After a time, the phone began to ring and Charlie's voice came onto the machine again. When I picked it up he sounded considerably calmer than before.

'I'm at the gate now,' he said. 'I'm sorry if I was a little flustered earlier on. Airports always make me that way. Can't ever settle until I'm sitting right by the gate. Ray, listen, there's just one thing that occurred to me. Concerning our strategy.'

'Our strategy?'

'Yes, our overall strategy. Of course, you've realised, this isn't the time for little tweakings of the truth to show yourself in a better light. Absolutely not the time for the small self-aggrandising white lie. No, no. You're remembering, aren't you, why you were given this job in the first place. Ray, I'm depending on you to present yourself to Emily just as you are. So long as you do that, our strategy stays on course.'

'Well, look, I'm hardly on course here to come over like Emily's greatest hero . . .'

'Yes, you appreciate the situation and I'm grateful. But something's just occurred to me. There's just one thing, one little thing in your repertoire that won't quite do here. You see, Ray, she's got this idea that you have good musical taste.'

'Ah . . .'

'Just about the only time she ever uses *you* to belittle me is in this area of musical taste. It's the one respect in which you aren't absolutely perfect for your current assignment. So Ray, you've got to promise not to talk about this topic.'

'Oh, for God's sake . . .'

'Just do it for me, Ray. It's not much to ask. Just don't start going on about that . . . that croony nostalgia music she likes. And if *she* brings it up, then you just play it dumb. That's all I'm asking. Otherwise, you just be your natural self. Ray, I can count on you about this, can't I?'

'Well, I suppose so. This is all pretty theoretical anyway. I don't see us chatting about anything this evening.'

'Good! So that's settled. Now, let's move to your little problem. You'll be glad to hear I've been giving it some thought. And I've come up with a solution. Are you listening?'

'Yes, I'm listening.'

'There's this couple who keep coming round. Angela and Solly. They're okay, but if they weren't neighbours we wouldn't have much to do with them. Anyway they often

[63]

come round. You know, dropping in without warning, expecting a cup of tea. Now here's the point. They turn up at various times in the day when they've been taking Hendrix out.'

'Hendrix?'

'Hendrix is a smelly, uncontrollable, possibly homicidal Labrador. For Angela and Solly, of course, the foul creature's the child they never had. Or the one they haven't had yet, they're probably still young enough for real children. But no, they prefer darling, darling Hendrix. And when they call round, darling Hendrix routinely goes about demolishing the place as determinedly as any disaffected burglar. Down goes the standard lamp. Oh dear, never mind, darling, did you have a fright? You get the picture. Now listen. About a year ago, we had this coffee-table book, cost a fortune, full of arty pictures of young gay men posing in North African casbahs. Emily liked to keep it open at this particular page, she thought it went with the sofa. She'd go mad if you turned over the page. Anyway, about a year ago, Hendrix came in and chewed it all up. That's right, sank his teeth into all that glossy photography, went on to chew up about twenty pages in all before Mummy could persuade him to desist. You see why I'm telling you this, don't you?'

'Yes. That is, I see a hint of an escape route, but . . .'

'All right, I'll spell it out. This is what you tell Emily. The door went, you answered it, this couple are there with Hendrix tugging at the leash. They tell you they're Angela and Solly, good friends needing their cup of tea. You let them in, Hendrix runs wild, chews up the diary. It's utterly plausible. What's the matter? Why aren't you thanking me? Won't quite do for you, sir?'

'I'm very grateful, Charlie. I'm just thinking it through, that's all. Look, for one thing, what if these people really turn up? After Emily's home, I mean.'

'That's possible, I suppose. All I can say is you'd be very, very unlucky if such a thing happened. When I said they came round a lot, I meant maybe once a month at most. So stop picking holes and be grateful.'

'But Charlie, isn't it a little far-fetched that this dog would chew just the diary, and exactly those pages?'

I heard him sigh. 'I assumed you didn't need the rest of it spelt out. Naturally, you have to do the place over a bit. Knock over the standard lamp, spill sugar over the kitchen floor. You have to make it like Hendrix did this whirlwind job on the place. Look, they're calling the flight. I've got to go. I'll check in with you once I'm in Germany.'

While listening to Charlie, a feeling had come over me similar to the one I get when someone starts on about a dream they had, or the circumstances that led to the little bump on their car door. His plan was all very well – ingenious, even – but I couldn't see how it had to do with anything I was really likely to say or do when Emily got home, and I'd found myself getting more and more impatient. But once Charlie had gone, I found his call had had a kind of hypnotic effect on me. Even as my head was dismissing his idea as idiotic, my arms and legs were setting out to put his 'solution' into action.

I began by putting the standard lamp down on its side. I was careful not to bump anything with it, and I removed the shade first, putting it back on at a cocked angle only once the whole thing was arranged on the floor. Then I took down a vase from a bookshelf and laid it down on the rug, spreading around it the dried grasses that had been inside. Next I selected a good spot near the coffee table to 'knock over' the wastepaper basket. I went about my work in a strange, disembodied mode. I didn't believe any of it would achieve anything, but I was finding the whole procedure rather soothing. Then I remembered all this vandalism was supposed to relate to the diary, and went through into the kitchen.

After a little think, I took a bowl of sugar from a cupboard, placed it on the table not far from the purple notebook, and slowly tilted it until the sugar slid out. I had a bit of a job preventing the bowl rolling off the edge of the table, but in the end got it to stay put. By this time, the gnawing panic I'd been feeling had evaporated. I wasn't tranquil, exactly, but it now seemed silly to have got myself in the state I had.

I went back to the living room, lay down on the sofa and picked up the Jane Austen book. After a few lines, I felt a huge tiredness coming over me and before I knew it, I was slipping into sleep once more.

I was woken up by the phone. When Emily's voice came on the machine, I sat up and answered it.

'Oh goody, Raymond, you *are* there. How are you, darling? How are you feeling now? Have you managed to relax?'

I assured her I had, that in fact I'd been sleeping.

'Oh what a pity! You probably haven't been sleeping properly for weeks, and now just when you finally get a moment's escape, I go and disturb you! I'm so sorry! And I'm sorry too, Ray, I'm going to have to disappoint you. There's an absolute crisis on here and I won't be able to get home quite as quickly as I'd hoped. In fact, I'm going to be another hour at least. You'll be able to hold out, won't you?'

I reiterated how relaxed and happy I was feeling.

'Yes, you do sound really stable now. I'm so sorry, Raymond, but I've got to go and sort this out. Help yourself to anything and everything. Goodbye, darling.'

I put down the phone and stretched my arms. The light was starting to fade now, so I went about the apartment switching on lights. Then I contemplated my 'wrecked' living room, and the more I looked at it, the more it seemed overwhelmingly contrived. The sense of panic began to grow once more in my stomach.

The phone went again, and this time it was Charlie. He was, he told me, beside the luggage carousel at Frankfurt airport.

'They're taking bloody ages. We haven't had a single bag come down yet. How are you making out over there? Madam not home yet?'

'No, not yet. Look, Charlie, that plan of yours. It's not going to work.'

'What do you mean, it's not going to work? Don't tell me you've been twiddling your thumbs all this time mulling it over.'

'I've done as you suggested. I've messed the place up, but it doesn't look convincing. It just doesn't look like a dog's been here. It just looks like an art exhibition.'

He was silent for a moment, perhaps concentrating on the carousel. Then he said: 'I can understand your problem. It's someone else's property. You're bound to be inhibited. So listen, I'm going to name a few items I'd dearly love to see damaged. Are you listening, Ray? I *want* the following things ruined. That stupid china ox thing. It's by the CD player. That's a present from David bloody Corey after his trip to Lagos. You can smash that up for a start. In fact, I don't care what you destroy. Destroy everything!'

'Charlie, I think you need to calm down.'

'Okay, okay. But that apartment's full of junk. Just like our marriage right now. Full of tired junk. That spongy red sofa, you know the one I mean, Ray?'

'Yes. Actually I fell asleep on it just now.'

'That should have been in a skip ages ago. Why don't you rip open the covering and throw the stuffing around.'

'Charlie, you have to get a grip. In fact, it occurs to me you're not trying to help me at all. You're just using me as a tool to express your rage and frustration . . .'

'Oh shut up with that bollocks! Of course I'm trying to help you. And of course my plan's a good one. I guarantee it'll work. Emily hates that dog, she hates Angela and Solly, so she'll seize any opportunity to hate them even more. Listen.' His voice suddenly dropped to a near-whisper. 'I'll give you the big tip. The secret ingredient that'll ensure she's convinced. I should have thought of this before. How much time do you have left?'

'Another hour or so . . .'

[68]

'Good. Listen carefully. Smell. That's right. You make that place smell of dog. From the moment she walks in, she'll register it, even if it's only subliminally. Then she steps into the room, notices darling David's china ox smashed up on the floor, the stuffing from that foul red sofa all over . . .'

'Now look, I didn't say I'd . . .'

'Just listen! She sees all the wreckage, and immediately, consciously or unconsciously, she'll make the connection with the dog smell. The whole scene with Hendrix will flash vividly through her head, even before you've said a word to her. That's the beauty of it!'

'You're havering, Charlie. Okay, so how do I make your home pong of dog?'

'I know exactly how you create a dog smell.' His voice was still an excited whisper. 'I know exactly how you do it, because me and Tony Barton used to do it in the Lower Sixth. He had a recipe, but I refined it.'

'But why?'

'Why? Because it stank more like cabbage than dog, that's why.'

'No, I meant why would you . . . Look, never mind. You might as well tell me, so long as it doesn't involve going out and buying a chemistry set.'

'Good. You're coming round to it. Get a pen, Ray. Write this down. Ah, here it comes at last.' He must have put the phone in his pocket, because for the next few moments I listened to womb noises. Then he came back and said:

'I have to go now. So write this down. Are you ready? The middle-sized saucepan. It's probably on the stove already. Put about a pint of water in it. Add two beef stock cubes, one dessertspoon of cumin, one tablespoon of paprika, two tablespoons of vinegar, a generous lot of bay leaves. Got that? Now you put in there a leather shoe or boot, upside down, so the sole's not actually immersed in the liquid. That's so you don't get any hint of burning rubber. Then you turn on the gas, bring the concoction to the boil, let it sit there simmering. Pretty soon, you'll notice the smell. It's not an awful smell. Tony Barton's original recipe involved garden slugs, but this one's much more subtle. Just like a smelly dog. I know, you're going to ask me where to find the ingredients. All the herbs and stuff are in the kitchen cupboards. If you go to the understairs cupboard, you'll find a discarded pair of boots in there. Not the wellingtons. I mean the battered-up pair, they're more like built-up shoes. I used to wear them all the time on the common. They've had it and they're waiting for the heave. Take one of those. What's the matter? Look, Ray, you just do this, okay? Save yourself. Because I'm telling you, an angry Emily is no joke. I've got to go now. Oh, and remember. No showing off your wonderful musical knowledge.'

Perhaps it was simply the effect of receiving a clear set of instructions, however dubious: when I put the phone down, a detached, business-like mood had come over me. I could see clearly just what I needed to do. I went into the kitchen and switched on the lights. Sure enough, the 'middle-sized' saucepan was sitting on the cooker, awaiting its next task. I filled it to halfway with water, and put it back on the hob. Even as I was doing this, I realised there was something else I had to establish before proceeding any further: namely, the precise amount of time I had to complete my work. I went into the living room, picked up the phone, and called Emily's work number.

I got her assistant, who told me Emily was in a meeting. I insisted, in a tone that balanced geniality with resolution, that she bring Emily out of her meeting, 'if indeed she is in one at all'. The next moment, Emily was on the line.

'What is it, Raymond? What's happened?'

'Nothing's happened. I'm just calling to find out how you are.'

'Ray, you sound odd. What is it?'

'What do you mean, I sound odd? I just called to establish when to expect you back. I know you regard me as a layabout, but I still appreciate a timetable of sorts.'

'Raymond, there's no need to get cross like that. Now let me see. It's going to be another hour . . . Maybe an hour and a half. I'm awfully sorry, but there's a real crisis on here . . .'

'One hour to ninety minutes. That's fine. That's all I need to know. Okay, I'll see you soon. You can get back to your business now.'

She might have been about to say something else, but I hung up and strode back into the kitchen, determined not to let my decisive mood evaporate. In fact, I was beginning to feel distinctly exhilarated, and I couldn't understand at all how I'd allowed myself to get into such a state of despondency earlier on. I went through the cupboards and lined up, in a neat row beside the hob, all the herbs and spices I needed. Then I measured them out into the water, gave a quick stir, and went off to find the boot.

The understairs cupboard was hiding a whole heap of sorry-looking footwear. After a few moments of rummaging, I discovered what was certainly one of the boots Charlie had prescribed – a particularly exhausted specimen with ancient mud encrusted along the rim of its heel. Holding it with fingertips, I took it back to the kitchen and placed it carefully in the water with the sole facing up to the ceiling. Then I lit a medium flame under the pan, sat down at the table and waited for the water to heat. When the phone rang again, I felt reluctant to abandon the saucepan, but then I heard Charlie on the machine going on and on. So I eventually turned the flame down low and went to answer him.

'What were you saying?' I asked. 'It sounded particularly self-pitying, but I was busy so I missed it.'

'I'm at the hotel. It's only a three-star. Can you believe the cheek! A big company like them! And it's a poxy little room too!'

'But you're only there for a couple of nights . . . '

'Listen, Ray, there's something I wasn't entirely honest about earlier. It's not fair on you. After all, you're doing me a favour, you're doing your best for me, trying to heal things with Emily, and here I am, being less than frank with you.'

'If you're talking about the recipe for the dog smell, it's too late. I've got it all going. I suppose I might be able to add an extra herb or something . . .'

'If I wasn't straight with you before, that's because I wasn't being straight with myself. But now I've come away, I've been able to think more clearly. Ray, I told you there wasn't anyone else, but that's not strictly true. There's this girl. Yes, she *is* a girl, early thirties at most. She's very concerned about education in the developing world, and fairer global trade. It wasn't really a sexual attraction thing, that was just a kind of by-product. It was her untarnished idealism. It reminded me of how we all were once. You remember that, Ray?'

'I'm sorry, Charlie, but I don't remember you ever being especially idealistic. In fact, you were always utterly selfish and hedonistic . . .'

'Okay, maybe we were all decadent slobs back then, the lot of us. But there's always been this other person, somewhere inside of me, wanting to come out. That's what drew me to her . . .'

'Charlie, when was this? When did this happen?'

'When did what happen?'

'This affair.'

'There was no affair! I didn't have sex with her, nothing. I didn't even have lunch with her. I just . . . I just made sure I kept seeing her.'

'What do you mean, kept seeing her?' I'd drifted back into the kitchen by this time and was gazing at my concoction.

'Well, I kept seeing her,' he said. 'I kept making appointments to see her.'

'You mean, she's a call girl.'

'No, no, I told you, we've never had sex. No, she's a dentist. I kept going back, kept making things up about a pain here, discomfort of the gums there. You know, I spun it out. And of course, in the end, Emily guessed.' For a second, Charlie seemed to be choking back a sob. Then the dam burst. 'She found out . . . she found out . . . because I was flossing so much!' He was now half-shrieking. 'She said, you *never, ever* floss your teeth that much!'

'But that doesn't make sense. If you look after your teeth more, you've less reason to go back to her . . .'

'Who cares if it makes sense? I just wanted to please her!'

'Look, Charlie, you didn't go out with her, you didn't have sex with her, what's the issue?'

'The issue is, I so wanted someone like that, someone who'd bring out this other me, the one that's been trapped inside . . .'

'Charlie, listen to me. Since the last time you called, I've pulled myself together considerably. And quite frankly, I think you should pull yourself together too. We can discuss all of this when you get back. But Emily will be here in an hour or so, and I've got to have everything ready. I'm on top of things here now, Charlie. I suppose you can tell that from my voice.'

'Fucking fantastic! You're on top of things. Great! Some fucking friend . . .'

'Charlie, I think you're upset because you don't like your hotel. But you should pull yourself together. Get things in perspective. And take heart. I'm on top of things here. I'll sort out the dog business, then I'll play my part up to the hilt for you. Emily, I'll say. Emily, just look at me, just look how pathetic I am. The truth is, most people are just as pathetic. But Charlie, he's different. Charlie is in a different league.'

'You can't say that. That sounds completely unnatural.'

'Of course I won't put it literally like that, idiot. Look, just leave it to me. I've got the whole situation under control. So calm down. Now I've got to go.'

I put the phone down and examined the pot. The liquid had now come to the boil and there was a lot of steam about, but as yet no real smell of any sort. I adjusted the flame until everything was bubbling nicely. It was around this point I was overcome by a craving for some fresh air, and since I hadn't yet investigated their roof terrace, I opened the kitchen door and stepped out.

It was surprisingly balmy for an English evening in early June. Only a little bite in the breeze told me I wasn't back in Spain. The sky wasn't fully dark yet, but was already filling with stars. Beyond the wall that marked the end of the terrace, I could see for miles around the windows and back yards of the neighbouring properties. A lot of the windows were lit, and the ones in the distance, if you narrowed your eyes, looked almost like an extension of the stars. This roof terrace wasn't large, but there was definitely something romantic about it. You could imagine a couple, in the midst of busy city lives, coming out here on a warm evening and strolling around the potted shrubs, in each other's arms, swapping stories about their day.

I could have stayed out there a lot longer, but I was afraid of losing my momentum. I went back into the kitchen, and walking past the bubbling pot, paused at the threshold of the living room to survey my earlier work. The big mistake, it struck me, lay in my complete failure to consider the task from the perspective of a creature like

Hendrix. The key, I now realised, was to immerse myself within Hendrix's spirit and vision.

Once I'd started on this tack, I saw not only the inadequacy of my previous efforts, but how hopeless most of Charlie's suggestions had been. Why would an over-lively dog extract a little ox ornament from the midst of hi-fi equipment and smash it? And the idea of cutting open the sofa and throwing around the stuffing was idiotic. Hendrix would need razor teeth to achieve an effect like that. The capsized sugar bowl in the kitchen was fine, but the living room, I realised, would have to be re-conceptualised from scratch.

I went into the room in a crouched posture, so as to see it from something like Hendrix's eyeline. Immediately, the glossy magazines piled up on the coffee table revealed themselves as an obvious target, and so I pushed them off the surface along a trajectory consistent with a shove from a rampant muzzle. The way the magazines landed on the floor looked satisfyingly authentic. Encouraged, I knelt down, opened one of the magazines and scrunched up a page in a manner, I hoped, would find an echo when eventually Emily came across the diary. But this time the result was disappointing: too obviously the work of a human hand rather than canine teeth. I'd fallen into my earlier error again: I'd not merged sufficiently with Hendrix.

So I got down on all fours, and lowering my head towards the same magazine, sank my teeth into the pages. The taste was perfumy, and not at all unpleasant. I opened a second fallen magazine near its centre and began to repeat the procedure. The ideal technique, I began to gather, was not unlike the one needed in those fairground games where you try to bite apples bobbing in water without using your hands. What worked best was a light, chewing motion, the jaws moving flexibly all the time: this would cause the pages to ruffle up and crease nicely. Too focused a bite, on the other hand, simply 'stapled' pages together to no great effect.

I think it was because I'd become so absorbed in these finer points that I didn't become aware sooner of Emily standing out in the hall, watching me from just beyond the doorway. Once I did realise she was there, my first feeling wasn't one of panic or embarrassment, but of hurt that she should be standing there like that without having announced her arrival in some way. In fact, when I remembered how I'd gone to the trouble of calling her office only several minutes earlier precisely to pre-empt the sort of situation now engulfing me, I felt the victim of a deliberate deception. Perhaps that was why my first visible response was simply to give a weary sigh without making any attempt to abandon my all-fours posture. My sigh brought Emily into the room, and she laid a hand very gently on my back. I'm not sure if she actually knelt down, but her face seemed close to mine as she said:

'Raymond, I'm back. So let's just sit down, shall we?'

She was easing me up onto my feet, and I had to resist the urge to shake her off.

'You know, it's odd,' I said. 'No more than a few minutes ago, you were about to go into a meeting.'

'I was, yes. But after your phone call, I realised the priority was to come back.'

[77]

'What do you mean, priority? Emily, please, you don't have to keep holding my arm like that, I'm not about to topple over. What do you mean, a priority to come back?'

'Your phone call. I recognised it for what it was. A cry for help.'

'It was nothing of the sort. I was just trying to . . .' I trailed off, because I noticed Emily was looking around the room with an expression of wonder.

'Oh, Raymond,' she muttered, almost to herself.

'I suppose I was being a little clumsy earlier on. I would have tidied up, except you came back early.'

I reached down to the fallen standard lamp, but Emily restrained me.

'It doesn't matter, Ray. It really doesn't matter at all. We can sort it all out together later. You just sit down now and relax.'

'Look, Emily, I realise it's your own home and all that. But why did you creep in so quietly?'

'I didn't creep in, darling. I called when I came in, but you didn't seem to be here. So I just popped into the loo and when I came out, well, there you were after all. But why go over it? None of it matters. I'm here now, and we can have a relaxing evening together. Please do sit down, Raymond. I'll make some tea.'

She was already going towards the kitchen as she said this. I was fiddling with the shade of the standard lamp and so it took me a moment to remember what was in there – by which time it was too late. I listened for her reaction, but there was only silence. Eventually I put down the lampshade and made my way to the kitchen doorway.

The saucepan was still bubbling away nicely, the steam rising around the upheld sole of the boot. The smell, which I'd barely registered until this point, was much more obvious in the kitchen itself. It was pungent, sure enough, and vaguely curryish. More than anything else, it conjured up those times you yank your foot out of a boot after a long sweaty hike.

Emily was standing a few paces back from the cooker, craning her neck to get as good a view of the pot as possible from a safe distance. She seemed absorbed by the sight of it, and when I gave a small laugh to announce my presence, she didn't shift her gaze, let alone turn around.

I squeezed past her and sat down at the kitchen table. Eventually, she turned to me with a kindly smile. 'It was a terribly sweet thought, Raymond.'

Then, as though against her will, her gaze was pulled back to the cooker.

I could see in front of me the tipped-up sugar bowl – and the diary – and a huge feeling of weariness came over me. Everything felt suddenly overwhelming, and I decided the only way forward was to stop all the games and come clean. Taking a deep breath, I said:

'Look, Emily. Things might look a little odd here. But it was all because of this diary of yours. This one here.' I opened it to the damaged page and showed her. 'It was really very wrong of me, and I'm truly sorry. But I happened to open it, and then, well, I happened to scrunch up the page. Like this . . .' I mimicked a less venomous version of my earlier action, then looked at her.

To my astonishment, she gave the diary no more than a

cursory glance before turning back to the pot, saying: 'Oh, that's just a jotter. Nothing private. Don't you worry about it, Ray.' Then she moved a step closer to the saucepan to study it all the better.

'What do you mean? What do you mean, don't worry about it? How can you say that?'

'What's the matter, Raymond? It's just something to jot down stuff I might forget.'

'But Charlie told me you'd go ballistic!' My sense of outrage was now being added to by the fact that Emily had obviously forgotten what she'd been writing about me.

'Really? Charlie told you I'd be angry?'

'Yes! In fact, he said you'd once told him you'd saw his balls off if he ever peeked inside this little book!'

I wasn't sure if Emily's puzzled look was due to what I was saying, or still left over from gazing at the saucepan. She sat down next to me and thought for a moment.

'No,' she said, eventually. 'That was about something else. I remember it clearly now. About this time last year, Charlie got despondent about something and asked what I'd do if he committed suicide. He was just testing me, he's far too chicken to try anything like that. But he asked, so I told him if he did anything like that I'd saw his balls off. That's the only time I've said that to him. I mean, it's not like a refrain on my part.'

'I don't get this. If he committed suicide, you'd do that to him? Afterwards?'

'It was just a figure of speech, Raymond. I was just trying to express how much I'd dislike him topping himself. I was making him feel valued.'

'You're missing my point. If you do it afterwards, it's not really a disincentive, is it? Or maybe you're right, it would be . . .'

'Raymond, let's forget it. Let's forget all of this. There's a lamb casserole from yesterday, there's over half of it left. It was pretty good last night, and it'll be even better tonight. And we can open a nice bottle of Bordeaux. It was awfully sweet of you to start preparing something for us. But the casserole's probably the thing for tonight, don't you think?'

All attempts to explain now seemed beyond me. 'Okay, okay. Lamb casserole. Terrific. Yes, yes.'

'So . . . we can put *this* away for now?'

'Yes, yes. Please do. Please put it away.'

I got up and went into the living room – which of course was still a mess, but I no longer had the energy to start tidying. Instead, I lay down on the sofa and stared at the ceiling. At one point, I was aware of Emily coming into the room, and I thought she'd gone through to the hall, but then I realised she was crouched in the far corner, fiddling with the hi-fi. The next thing, the room filled with lush strings, bluesy horns, and Sarah Vaughan singing 'Lover Man'.

A sense of relief and comfort washed over me. Nodding to the slow beat, I closed my eyes, remembering how all those years ago, in her college room, she and I had argued for over an hour about whether Billie Holiday always sang this song better than Sarah Vaughan.

Emily touched my shoulder and handed me a glass of red wine. She had a frilly apron on over her business suit, and was holding a glass for herself. She sat down at the far end of the sofa, next to my feet, and took a sip. Then she turned down the volume a little with her remote.

'It's been an awful day,' she said. 'I don't mean just work, which is a total mess. I mean Charlie going, everything. Don't imagine it doesn't hurt me, to have him go off abroad like that when we haven't made up. Then to cap it all, you finally go and tip over the edge.' She gave a long sigh.

'No, really, Emily, it's not as bad as that. For a start, Charlie thinks the world of you. And as for me, I'm fine. I'm really fine.'

'Bollocks.'

'No, really. I feel fine . . .'

'I meant about Charlie thinking the world of me.'

'Oh, I see. Well, if you think that's bollocks, you couldn't be more wrong. In fact, I know Charlie loves you more than ever.'

'How can you know that, Raymond?'

'I know because . . . well, for a start he more or less told me so, when we were having lunch. And even if he didn't spell it out, I can tell. Look, Emily, I know things are a bit tough right now. But you've got to hang onto the most important thing. Which is that he still loves you very much.'

She did another sigh. 'You know, I haven't listened to this record for ages. It's because of Charlie. If I put this sort of music on, he immediately starts groaning.'

We didn't speak for a few moments, but just listened to Sarah Vaughan. Then as an instrumental break started,

Emily said: 'I suppose, Raymond, you prefer her other version of this. The one she did with just piano and bass.'

I didn't reply, but just propped myself up a little more so as to sip my wine better.

'I bet you do,' she said. 'You prefer that other version. Don't you, Raymond?'

'Well,' I said, 'I really don't know. To tell you the truth, I don't remember the other version.'

I could feel Emily shift at the end of the sofa. 'You're kidding, Raymond.'

'It's funny, but I don't listen to this kind of stuff much these days. In fact, I've forgotten almost everything about it. I'm not even sure what song this is right now.' I did a little laugh, which perhaps didn't come out very well.

'What are you talking about?' She sounded suddenly cross. 'That's ridiculous. Short of having had a lobotomy, there's no way you could have forgotten.'

'Well. A lot of years have gone by. Things change.'

'What are you talking about?' There was now a hint of panic in her voice. 'Things can't change that much.'

I was pretty desperate to get off the subject. So I said: 'Pity things are such a mess at your work.'

Emily completely ignored this. 'So what are you saying? You're saying you don't like *this*? You want me to turn it off, is that it?'

'No, no, Emily, please, it's lovely. It . . . it brings back memories. Please, let's just get back to being quiet and relaxed, the way we were a minute ago.'

She did another sigh, and when she next spoke her voice was gentle again.

'I'm sorry, darling. I'd forgotten. That's the last thing you need, me yelling at you. I'm so sorry.'

'No, no, it's okay.' I heaved myself up to a sitting position. 'You know, Emily, Charlie's a decent guy. A very decent guy. And he loves you. You won't do better, you know.'

Emily shrugged and drank some more wine. 'You're probably right. And we're hardly young any more. We're as bad as one another. We should count ourselves lucky. But we never seem to be contented. I don't know why. Because when I stop and think about it, I realise I don't really want anyone else.'

For the next minute or so, she kept sipping her wine and listening to the music. Then she said: 'You know, Raymond, when you're at a party, at a dance. And it's maybe a slow dance, and you're with the person you really want to be with, and the rest of the room's supposed to vanish. But somehow it doesn't. It just doesn't. You know there's no one half as nice as the guy in your arms. And yet . . . well, there are all these people everywhere else in the room. They don't leave you alone. They keep shouting and waving and doing daft things just to attract your attention. "Oi! How can you be satisfied with that?! You can do much better! Look over here!" It's like they're shouting things like that all the time. And so it gets hopeless, you can't just dance quietly with your guy. Do you know what I mean, Raymond?'

I thought about it for a while, then said: 'Well, I'm not as lucky as you and Charlie. I don't have anyone special like you do. But yes, in some ways, I know just what you mean.

It's hard to know where to settle. What to settle to.'

'Bloody right. I wish they'd just lay off, all these gate-crashers. I wish they'd just lay off and let us get on with it.'

'You know, Emily, I wasn't kidding just now. Charlie thinks the world of you. He's so upset things haven't been going well between you.'

Her back was more or less turned to me, and she didn't say anything for a long time. Then Sarah Vaughan began her beautiful, perhaps excessively slow version of 'April in Paris', and Emily started up like Sarah had called her name. Then she turned to me and shook her head.

'I can't get over it, Ray. I can't get over how you don't listen to this kind of music any more. We used to play all these records back then. On that little record player Mum bought me before I came to university. How could you just forget?'

I got to my feet and walked over to the french doors, still holding my glass. When I looked out to the terrace, I realised my eyes had filled with tears. I opened the door and stepped outside so I could wipe them without Emily noticing, but then she was following right behind me, so maybe she noticed, I don't know.

The evening was pleasantly warm, and Sarah Vaughan and her band came drifting out onto the terrace. The stars were brighter than before, and the lights of the neighbourhood were still twinkling like an extension of the night sky.

'I love this song,' Emily said. 'I suppose you've forgotten this one too. But even if you've forgotten it, you can dance to it, can't you?'

'Yes. I suppose I can.'

'We could be like Fred Astaire and Ginger Rogers.'

'Yes, we could.'

We placed our wine glasses on the stone table and began to dance. We didn't dance especially well – we kept bumping our knees – but I held Emily close to me, and my senses filled with the texture of her clothes, her hair, her skin. Holding her like this, it occurred to me again how much weight she'd put on.

'You're right, Raymond,' she said, quietly in my ear. 'Charlie's all right. We should sort ourselves out.'

'Yes. You should.'

'You're a good friend, Raymond. What would we do without you?'

'If I'm a good friend, I'm glad. Because I'm not much good at anything else. In fact, I'm pretty useless, really.'

I felt a sharp tug on my shoulder.

'Don't say that,' she whispered. 'Don't talk like that.' Then a moment later, she said again: 'You're such a good friend, Raymond.'

This was Sarah Vaughan's 1954 version of 'April in Paris', with Clifford Brown on trumpet. So I knew it was a long track, at least eight minutes. I felt pleased about that, because I knew after the song ended, we wouldn't dance any more, but go in and eat the casserole. And for all I knew, Emily would re-consider what I'd done to her diary, and decide this time it wasn't such a trivial offence. What did I know? But for another few minutes at least, we were safe, and we kept dancing under the starlit sky.

[86]

MALVERN HILLS

I'D SPENT THE SPRING in London, and all in all, even if I hadn't achieved everything I'd set out to, it had been an exciting interlude. But with the weeks slipping by and summer getting closer, the old restlessness had started to return. For one thing, I was getting vaguely paranoid about running into any more of my former university friends. Wandering around Camden Town, or going through CDs I couldn't afford in West End megastores, I'd already had too many of them come up to me, asking how I was getting on since leaving the course to 'seek fame and fortune'. It's not that I was embarrassed to tell them what I'd been up to. It was just that – with a very few exceptions – none of them was capable of grasping what was or wasn't, for me at this particular point, a 'successful' few months.

As I've said, I hadn't achieved every goal I'd set my sights on, but then those goals had always been more like long-term targets. And all those auditions, even the really dreary ones, had been an invaluable experience. In almost every case, I'd taken something away with me, something I'd learned about the scene in London, or else about the music business in general.

Some of these auditions had been pretty professional affairs. You'd find yourself in a warehouse, or a converted garage block, and there'd be a manager, or maybe the girl-friend of a band member, taking your name, asking you to wait, offering you tea, while the sounds of the band, stop-ping and starting, thundered out from the adjoining space. But the majority of auditions happened at a much more shambolic level. In fact, when you saw the way most bands went about things, it was no mystery why the whole scene in London was dying on its feet. Time and again, I'd walk past rows of anonymous suburban terraces on the city out-skirts, carry my acoustic guitar up a staircase, and enter a stale-smelling flat with mattresses and sleeping bags all over the floor, and band members who mumbled and barely looked you in the eye. I'd sing and play while they stared emptily at me, till one of them might bring it to an end by saying something like: 'Yeah, well. Thanks anyway, but it's not quite our genre.'

I soon worked out that most of these guys were shy or plain awkward about the audition process, and that if I chatted to them about other things, they'd become a lot more relaxed. That's when I'd pick up all kinds of useful info: where the interesting clubs were, or the names of other bands in need of a guitarist. Or sometimes it was just a tip about a new act to check out. As I say, I never came away empty-handed.

On the whole, people really liked my guitar-playing, and a lot of them said my vocals would come in handy for harmonies. But it quickly emerged there were two fac-tors going against me. The first was that I didn't have equipment. A lot of bands were wanting someone with electric guitar, amps, speakers, preferably transport, ready to slot right into their gigging schedule. I was on foot with a fairly crappy acoustic. So no matter how much they liked my rhythm work or my voice, they'd no choice but to turn me away. This was fair enough.

Much harder to accept was the other main obstacle – and I have to say, I was completely surprised by this one. There was actually a problem about me writing my own songs. I couldn't believe it. There I'd be, in some dingy apartment, playing to a circle of blank faces, then at the end, after a silence that could go on for fifteen, thirty seconds, one of them would ask suspiciously: 'So whose number was that?' And when I said it was one of my own, you'd see the shutters coming down. There'd be little shrugs, shakes of the head, sly smiles exchanged, then they'd be giving me their rejection patter.

The umpteenth time this happened, I got so exasperated, I said: 'Look, I don't get this. Are you wanting to be a covers band for ever? And even if that's what you want to be, where do you think those songs come from in the first place? Yeah, that's right. Someone writes them!'

But the guy I was talking to stared at me vacantly, then said: 'No offence, mate. It's just that there are so many wankers going around writing songs.'

The stupidity of this position, which seemed to extend right across the London scene, was key to persuading me there was something if not utterly rotten, then at least extremely shallow and inauthentic about what was going down here, right at the grass-roots level, and that this was undoubtedly a reflection of what was happening in the music industry all the way up the ladder.

It was this realisation, and the fact that as the summer came closer I was running out of floors to sleep on, that made me feel for all the fascination of London – my university days looked grey by comparison – it would be good to take a break from the city. So I called up my sister, Maggie, who runs a cafe with her husband up in the Malvern Hills, and that's how it came to be decided I'd spend the summer with them.

Maggie's four years older and is always worrying about me, so I knew she'd be all for my coming up. In fact, I could tell she was glad to be getting the extra help. When I say her cafe is in the Malvern Hills, I don't mean it's in Great Malvern or down on the A road, but literally up there in the hills. It's an old Victorian house standing by itself facing the west side, so when the weather's nice, you can have your tea and cake out on the cafe terrace with a sweeping view over Herefordshire. Maggie and Geoff have to close the place in the winter, but in the summer it's always busy, mainly with the locals – who park their cars in the West of England car park a hundred yards below and come panting up the path in sandals and floral dresses – or else the walking brigade with their maps and serious gear.

Maggie said she and Geoff couldn't afford to pay me, which suited me just fine because it meant I couldn't be expected to work too hard for them. All the same, since I was getting bed and board, the understanding seemed to be that I'd be a third member of staff. It was all a bit unclear, and at the start, Geoff, in particular, seemed torn between giving me a kick up the arse for not doing enough, and apologising for asking me to do anything at all, like I was a guest. But things soon settled down to a pattern. The work was easy enough – I was especially good at making sandwiches – and I sometimes had to keep reminding myself of my main objective in coming out to the country in the first place: that's to say, I was going to write a brand-new batch of songs ready for my return to London in the autumn.

I'm naturally an early riser, but I quickly discovered that breakfast at the cafe was a nightmare, with customers wanting eggs done this way, toast like that, everything getting overcooked. So I made a point of never appearing until around eleven. While all the clatter was going on downstairs, I'd open the big bay window in my room, sit on the broad window sill and play my guitar looking out over miles and miles of countryside. There was a run of really clear mornings just after I arrived, and it was a glorious feeling, like I could see forever, and when I strummed my chords, they were ringing out across the whole nation. Only when I turned and stuck my head right out of the window would I get an aerial view of the cafe terrace below, and become aware of the people coming and going with their dogs and pushchairs.

I wasn't a stranger to this area. Maggie and I had grown up only a few miles away in Pershore and our parents had often brought us for walks on the hills. But I'd never been much up for it in those days, and as soon as I was old enough, I'd refused to go with them. That summer though,

I felt this was the most beautiful place in the world; that in many ways I'd come from and belonged to the hills. Maybe it was something to do with our parents having split up, the fact that for some time now, that little grey house opposite the hairdresser was no longer 'our' house. Whatever it was, this time round, instead of the claustrophobia I remembered from my childhood, I felt affection, even nostalgia, about the area.

I found myself wandering in the hills practically every day, sometimes with my guitar if I was sure it wouldn't rain. I liked in particular Table Hill and End Hill, at the north end of the range, which tend to get neglected by day-trippers. There I'd sometimes be lost in my thoughts for hours at a time without seeing a soul. It was like I was discovering the hills for the first time, and I could almost taste the ideas for new songs welling up in my mind.

Working at the cafe, though, was another matter. I'd catch a voice, or see a face coming up to the counter while I was preparing a salad, that would jerk me back to an earlier part of my life. Old friends of my parents would come up and grill me about what I was up to, and I'd have to bluff until they decided to leave me in peace. Usually they'd sign off with something like: 'Well at least you're keeping busy,' nodding towards the sliced bread and tomatoes, before waddling back to their table with their cup and saucer. Or someone I'd known at school would come in and start talking to me in their new 'university' voice, maybe dissecting the latest Batman film in clever-clever language, or else starting on about the real causes of world poverty.

I didn't really mind any of this. In fact, some of these people I was genuinely quite glad to see. But there was one person who came into the cafe that summer, the instant I saw her, I felt myself freezing up, and by the time it occurred to me to escape into the kitchen, she'd already seen me.

This was Mrs Fraser – or Hag Fraser, as we used to call her. I recognised her as soon as she came in with a muddy little bulldog. I felt like telling her she couldn't bring the dog inside, though people always did that when they came to get things. Hag Fraser had been one of my teachers at school in Pershore. Thankfully she retired before I went into the sixth form, but in my memory her shadow falls over my entire school career. Her aside, school hadn't been that bad, but she'd had it in for me from the start, and when you're just eleven years old, there's nothing you can do to defend yourself from someone like her. Her tricks were the usual ones twisted teachers have, like asking me in lessons exactly the questions she sensed I wouldn't be able to answer, then making me stand up and getting the class to laugh at me. Later, it got more subtle. I remember once, when I was fourteen, a new teacher, a Mr Travis, had exchanged jokes with me in class. Not jokes against me, but like we were equals, and the class had laughed, and I'd felt good about it. But a couple of days later, I was going down the corridor and Mr Travis was coming the other way, talking with *her*, and as I came by she stopped me and gave me a complete bollocking about late homework or something. The point is she'd done this just to let Mr Travis know I was a 'troublemaker'; that if he'd thought for one moment I was one of the boys worthy of his respect, he was making a big mistake. Maybe it was because she was old, I don't know, but the other teachers never seemed to see through her. They all took whatever she said as gospel.

When Hag Fraser came in that day, it was obvious she remembered me, but she didn't smile or call me by name. She bought a cup of tea and a packet of Custard Creams, then took them outside to the terrace. I thought that was that. But then a while later, she came in again, put her empty cup and saucer down on the counter and said: 'Since you won't clear the table, I've brought these in myself.' She gave me a look that went on a second or two longer than was normal – her old if-only-I-could-swat-you look – then left.

All my hatred for the old dragon came back, and by the time Maggie came down a few minutes later, I was completely fuming. She saw it straight away and asked what was wrong. There were a few customers out on the terrace, but no one inside, so I started shouting, calling Hag Fraser every filthy name she deserved. Maggie got me to calm down, then said:

'Well, she's not anybody's teacher any more. She's just a sad old lady whose husband's gone and left her.'

'Not surprised.'

'But you have to feel a bit sorry for her. Just when she thought she could enjoy her retirement, she's left for a younger woman. And now she has to run that bed-and-breakfast by herself and people say the place is falling apart.'

This all cheered me up no end. I forgot about Hag Fraser soon after that, because a group came in and I had to make a lot of tuna salads. But a few days later when I was chatting to Geoff in the kitchen, I got a few more details from him; like how her husband of forty-odd years had gone off with his secretary; and how their hotel had got off to a reasonable start, but now all the gossip was of guests demanding their money back, or checking out within hours of arrival. I saw the place myself once when I was helping Maggie with the cash-and-carry and we drove past. Hag Fraser's hotel was right there on the Elgar Route, a fairly substantial granite house with an outsize sign saying 'Malvern Lodge'.

But I don't want to go on about Hag Fraser too much. I'm not obsessed with her or with her hotel. I'm only putting this all here now because of what happened later, once Tilo and Sonja came in.

Geoff had gone into Great Malvern that day, so it was just me and Maggie holding the fort. The main lunch rush was over, but at the point when the Krauts came in, we still had plenty going on. I'd clocked them in my mind as 'the Krauts' the moment I heard their accents. I wasn't being racist. If you have to stand behind a counter and remember who didn't want beetroot, who wanted extra bread, who gets what put on which bill, you've no choice but to turn all the customers into characters, give them names, pick out physical peculiarities. Donkey Face had a ploughman's and two coffees. Tuna mayo baguettes for Winston Churchill and his wife. That's how I was doing it. So Tilo and Sonja were 'the Krauts'.

It was very hot that afternoon, but most of the customers – being English – still wanted to sit outside on the
terrace, some of them even avoiding the parasols so they
could go bright red in the sun. But the Krauts decided to
sit indoors in the shade. They had on loose, camel-
coloured trousers, trainers and T-shirts, but somehow
looked smart, the way people from the continent often do.
I supposed they were in their forties, maybe early fifties – I
didn't pay too much attention at that stage. They ate their
lunch talking quietly to each other, and they seemed like
any pleasant, middle-aged couple from Europe. Then after
a while, the guy got up and started wandering about the
room, pausing to study an old faded photo Maggie has on
the wall, of the house as it was in 1915. Then he stretched
out his arms and said:

'Your countryside here is so wonderful! We have many
fine mountains in Switzerland. But what you have here is
different. They are hills. You call them hills. They have a
charm all their own because they are gentle and friendly.'

'Oh, you're from Switzerland,' Maggie said in her polite
voice. 'I've always wanted to go there. It sounds so fantastic, the Alps, the cable-cars.'

'Of course, our country has many beautiful features. But
here, in this spot, you have a special charm. We have
wanted to visit this part of England for so long. We always
talked of it, and now finally we are here!' He gave a hearty
laugh. 'So happy to be here!'

'That's splendid,' Maggie said. 'I do hope you enjoy it.
Are you here for long?'

'We have another three days before we must return to

our work. We have looked forward to coming here ever since we observed a wonderful documentary film many years ago, concerning Elgar. Evidently Elgar loved these hills and explored them thoroughly on his bicycle. And now we are finally here!'

Maggie chatted with him for a few minutes about places they'd already visited in England, what they should see in the local area, the usual stuff you were supposed to say to tourists. I'd heard it loads of times before, and I could do it myself more or less on automatic, so I started to tune out. I just took in that the Krauts were actually Swiss and that they were travelling around by hired car. He kept saying what a great place England was and how kind everyone had been, and made big laughing noises whenever Maggie said anything halfway jokey. But as I say, I'd tuned out, thinking they were just this fairly boring couple. I only started paying attention again a few moments later, when I noticed the way the guy kept trying to bring his wife into the conversation, and how she kept silent, her eyes fixed on her guidebook and behaving like she wasn't aware of any conversation at all. That's when I took a closer look at them.

They both had even, natural suntans, quite unlike the sweaty lobster looks of the locals outside, and despite their age, they were both slim and fit-looking. His hair was grey, but luxuriant, and he'd had it carefully groomed, though in a vaguely seventies style, a bit like the guys in Abba. Her hair was blonde, almost snowy white, and her face was stern-looking, with little lines etched around the mouth that spoilt what would otherwise have been the beautiful older woman look. So there he was, as I say, trying to bring her into the conversation.

'Of course, my wife enjoys Elgar greatly and so would be most curious to visit the house in which he was born.'

Silence.

Or: 'I am not a great fan of Paris, I must confess. I much prefer London. But Sonja here, she loves Paris.'

Nothing.

Each time he said something like this, he'd turn towards his wife in the corner, and Maggie would be obliged to look over to her, but the wife still wouldn't glance up from her book. The man didn't seem especially perturbed by this and went on talking cheerfully. Then he stretched out his arms again and said: 'If you will excuse me, I think I may for a moment go and admire your splendid scenery!'

He went outside, and we could see him walking around the terrace. Then he disappeared out of our view. The wife was still there in the corner, reading her guidebook, and after a while Maggie went over to her table and began clearing up. The woman ignored her completely until my sister picked up a plate with a tiny bit of roll still left on it. Then suddenly she slammed down her book and said, far more loudly than necessary: 'I have not finished yet!'

Maggie apologised and left her with her piece of roll – which I noticed the woman made no move to touch. Maggie looked at me as she came past and I gave her a shrug. Then a few moments later, my sister asked the woman, very nicely, if there was anything else she'd like.

'No. I want nothing else.'

I could tell from her tone she should be left alone, but

with Maggie it was a kind of reflex. She asked, like she really wanted to know: 'Was everything all right?'

For at least five or six seconds, the woman went on reading, like she hadn't heard. Then she put down her book again and glared at my sister.

'Since you ask,' she said, 'I shall tell you. The food was perfectly okay. Better than in many of the awful places you have around here. However, we waited thirty-five minutes simply to be served a sandwich and a salad. Thirty-five minutes.'

I now realised this woman was livid with anger. Not the sort that suddenly hits you, then drains away. No, this woman, I could tell, had been in a kind of white heat for some time. It's the sort of anger that arrives and stays put, at a constant level, like a bad headache, never quite peaking and refusing to find a proper outlet. Maggie's always so even-tempered she couldn't recognise the symptoms, and probably thought the woman was complaining in a more or less rational way. Because she apologised and started to say: 'But you see, when there's a big rush like we had earlier . . .'

'Surely you get it every day, no? Is that not so? Every day, in the summer, when the weather is fine, there is just such a big rush? Well? So why can't you be ready? Something that happens every day and it surprises you. Is that what you are telling me?'

The woman had been glaring at my sister, but as I came out from behind the counter to stand beside Maggie, she transferred her gaze to me. And maybe it was to do with the expression I had on my face, I could see her anger go up a couple more notches. Maggie turned and looked at me, and began gently to push me away, but I resisted, and kept gazing at the woman. I wanted her to know it wasn't just her and Maggie in this. God knows where this would have got us, but at that moment the husband came back in.

'Such a marvellous view! A marvellous view, a marvellous lunch, a marvellous country!'

I waited for him to sense what he'd walked into, but if he noticed, he showed no sign of taking it into account. He smiled at his wife and said, presumably for our benefit in English: 'Sonja, you really must go and have a look. Just walk to the end of the little path out there!'

She said something in German, then went back to her book. He came further into the room and said to us:

'We had considered driving on to Wales this afternoon. But your Malvern Hills are so wonderful, I really think we might stay here in this district for the remaining three days of our vacation. If Sonja agrees, I will be overjoyed!'

He looked at his wife, who shrugged and said something else in German, to which he laughed his loud, open laugh.

'Good! She agrees! So it is settled. We will no longer drive to Wales. We will hang out here in your district for the next three days!'

He beamed at us, and Maggie said something encouraging. I was relieved to see the wife putting her book away and getting ready to leave. The man, too, went to the table, picked up a small rucksack and put it on his shoulder. Then he said to Maggie:

'I wonder. Is there by any chance a small hotel you can

recommend for us nearby? Nothing too expensive, but comfortable and pleasant. And if possible, with something of the English flavour!'

Maggie was a bit stumped by this and delayed her answer by saying something meaningless like: 'What sort of place did you want?' But I said quickly:

'The best place around here is Mrs Fraser's. It's just down along the road to Worcester. It's called Malvern Lodge.'

'The Malvern Lodge! That sounds just the ticket!'

Maggie turned away disapprovingly and pretended to be clearing away more things while I gave them all the details on how to find Hag Fraser's hotel. Then the couple left, the guy thanking us with big smiles, the woman not giving a backward glance.

My sister gave me a weary look and shook her head. I just laughed and said:

'You've got to admit, that woman and Hag Fraser really deserve one another. It was just too good an opportunity to miss.'

'It's all very well for you to amuse yourself like that,' Maggie said, pushing past me to the kitchen. 'I have to live here.'

'So what? Look, you'll never see those Krauts again. And if Hag Fraser finds out we've been recommending her place to passing tourists, she's hardly going to complain, is she?'

Maggie shook her head, but there was more of a smile about it this time.

*

The cafe got quieter after that, then Geoff came back, so I went off upstairs, feeling I'd done more than my share for the time being. Up in my room, I sat at the bay window with my guitar and for a while got engrossed in a song I was halfway through writing. But then – and it seemed like no time – I could hear the afternoon tea rush starting downstairs. If it got really mad, like it usually did, Maggie was bound to ask me to come down – which really wouldn't be fair, given how much I'd done already. So I decided the best thing would be for me to slip out to the hills and continue my work there.

I left the back way without encountering anyone, and immediately felt glad to be out in the open. It was pretty warm though, especially carrying a guitar case, and I was glad of the breeze.

I was heading for a particular spot I'd discovered the previous week. To get there you climbed a steep path behind the house, then walked a few minutes along a more gradual incline till you came to this bench. It's one I'd chosen carefully, not just because of the fantastic view, but because it wasn't at one of those junctions in the paths where people with exhausted children come staggering up and sit next to you. On the other hand it wasn't completely isolated, and every now and then, a walker would pass by, saying 'Hi!' in the way they do, maybe adding some quip about my guitar, all without breaking stride. I didn't mind this at all. It was kind of like having an audience and not having one, and it gave my imagination just that little edge it needed.

I'd been there on my bench for maybe half an hour when I became aware that some walkers, who'd just gone past with the usual short greeting, had now stopped several yards away and were watching me. This did rather annoy me, and I said, a little sarcastically:

'It's okay. You don't have to toss me any money.'

This was answered by a big hearty laugh which I recognised, and I looked up to see the Krauts coming back towards the bench.

The possibility flashed through my mind that they'd gone to Hag Fraser's, realised I'd pulled a fast one on them, and were now coming to get even with me. But then I saw that not only the guy, but the woman too, was smiling cheerfully. They retraced their steps till they were standing in front of me, and since by this time the sun was falling, they appeared for a moment as two silhouettes, the big afternoon sky behind them. Then they came closer and I could see they were both gazing at my guitar – which I'd continued to play – with a look of happy amazement, the way people gaze at a baby. Even more astonishing, the woman was tapping her foot to my beat. I got self-conscious and stopped.

'Hey, carry on!' the woman said. 'It's really good what you play there.'

'Yes,' the husband said, 'wonderful! We heard it from a distance.' He pointed. 'We were right up there, on that ridge, and I said to Sonja, I can hear music.'

'Singing too,' the woman said. 'I said to Tilo, listen, there is singing somewhere. And I was right, yes? You were singing also a moment ago.'

I couldn't quite accept that this smiling woman was the same one who'd given us such a hard time at lunch, and I looked at them again carefully, in case this was a different couple altogether. But they were in the same clothes, and though the man's Abba-style hair had come undone a bit in the wind, there was no mistaking it. In any case, the next moment, he said:

'I believe you are the gentleman who served us lunch in the delightful restaurant.'

I agreed I was. Then the woman said:

'That melody you were singing a moment ago. We heard it up there, just in the wind at first. I loved the way it fell at the end of each line.'

'Thanks,' I said. 'It's something I'm working on. Not finished yet.'

'Your own composition? Then you must be very gifted! Please do sing your melody again, as you were before.'

'You know,' the guy said, 'when you come to record your song, you must tell the producer *this* is how you want it to sound. Like this!' He gestured behind him at Herefordshire stretched out before us. 'You must tell him this is the sound, the aural environment you require. Then the listener will hear your song as we heard it today, caught in the wind as we descend the slope of the hill . . .'

'But a little more clearly, of course,' the woman said. 'Or else the listener will not catch the words. But Tilo is correct. There must be a suggestion of outdoors. Of air, of echo.'

They seemed on the verge of getting carried away, like they'd just come across another Elgar in the hills. Despite my initial suspicions, I couldn't help but warm to them.

'Well,' I said, 'since I wrote most of the song up here, it's no wonder there's something of this place in it.'

'Yes, yes,' they both said together, nodding. Then the woman said: 'You must not be shy. Please share your music with us. It sounded wonderful.'

'All right,' I said, playing a little doodle. 'All right, I'll sing you a song, if you really want me to. Not the one I haven't finished. Another one. But look, I can't do it with you two standing right over me like this.'

'Of course,' Tilo said. 'We are being so inconsiderate. Sonja and I have had to perform in so many strange and difficult conditions, we become insensitive to the needs of another musician.'

He looked around and sat down on a patch of stubbly grass near the path, his back to me and facing the view. Sonja gave me an encouraging smile, then sat down beside him. Immediately, he put an arm around her shoulders, she leaned towards him, then it was almost like I wasn't there any more, and they were having an intimate lovey-dovey moment gazing over the late-afternoon countryside.

'Okay, here goes,' I said, and went into the song I usually open with at auditions. I aimed my voice at the horizon but kept glancing at Tilo and Sonja. Though I couldn't see their faces, the whole way they remained snuggled up to each other with no hint of restlessness told me they were enjoying what they were hearing. When I finished, they turned to me with big smiles and applauded, sending echoes around the hills.

'Fantastic!' Sonja said. 'So talented!'

'Splendid, splendid,' Tilo was saying.

I felt a little embarrassed by this and pretended to be

absorbed in some guitar work. When I eventually looked up again, they were still sitting on the ground, but had now shifted their positions so they could see me.

'So you're musicians?' I asked. 'I mean, *professional* musicians?'

'Yes,' said Tilo, 'I suppose you could call us professionals. Sonja and I, we perform as a duo. In hotels, restaurants. At weddings, at parties. All over Europe, though we like best to work in Switzerland and Austria. We make our living this way, so yes, we are professionals.'

'But first and foremost,' Sonja said, 'we play because we believe in the music. I can see it is the same for you.'

'If I stopped believing in my music,' I said, 'I'd stop, just like that.' Then I added: 'I'd really like to do it professionally. It must be a good life.'

'Oh yes, it's a good life,' said Tilo. 'We're very lucky we are able to do what we do.'

'Look,' I said, maybe a little suddenly. 'Did you go to that hotel I told you about?'

'How very rude of us!' Tilo exclaimed. 'We were so taken by your music, we forgot completely to thank you. Yes, we went there and it is just the ticket. Fortunately there were still vacancies.'

'It's just what we wanted,' said Sonja. 'Thank you.'

I pretended again to become absorbed in my chords. Then I said as casually as I could: 'Come to think of it, there's this other hotel I know. I think it's better than Malvern Lodge. I think you should change.'

'Oh, but we're quite settled now,' said Tilo. 'We have unpacked our things, and besides, it's just what we need.'

'Yeah, but . . . Well, the thing is, earlier on, when you asked me about a hotel, I didn't know you were musicians. I thought you were bankers or something.'

They both burst out laughing, like I'd made a fantastic joke. Then Tilo said:

'No, no, we're not bankers. Though there have been many times we wished we were!'

'What I'm saying,' I said, 'is there are other hotels much more geared, you know, to artistic types. It's hard when strangers ask you to recommend a hotel, before you know what sort of people they are.'

'It's kind of you to worry,' said Tilo. 'But please, don't do so any longer. What we have is perfect. Besides, people are not so different. Bankers, musicians, we all in the end want the same things from life.'

'You know, I'm not sure that is so true,' Sonja said. 'Our young friend here, you see he doesn't look for a job in a bank. His dreams are different.'

'Perhaps you are right, Sonja. All the same, the present hotel is fine for us.'

I leant over the strings and practised another little phrase to myself, and for a few seconds nobody spoke. Then I asked: 'So what sort of music do you guys play?'

Tilo shrugged. 'Sonja and I play a number of instruments between us. We both play keyboards. I am fond of the clarinet. Sonja is a very fine violinist, and also a splendid singer. I suppose what we like to do best is to perform our traditional Swiss folk music, but in a contemporary manner. Sometimes even what you might call a radical manner. We take inspiration from great composers who took a similar path. Janáček, for instance. Your own Vaughan Williams.'

'But that kind of music', Sonja said, 'we don't play so much now.'

They exchanged glances with what I thought was just a hint of tension. Then Tilo's usual smile was back on his face.

'Yes, as Sonja points out, in this real world, much of the time, we must play what our audience is most likely to appreciate. So we perform many hits. Beatles, the Carpenters. Some more recent songs. This is perfectly satisfying.'

'What about Abba?' I asked on an impulse, then immediately regretted it. But Tilo didn't seem to sense any mockery.

'Yes, indeed, we do some Abba. "Dancing Queen". That one always goes down well. In fact, it is on "Dancing Queen" I actually do a little singing myself, a little harmony part. Sonja will tell you I have the most terrible voice. So we must make sure to perform this song only when our customers are right in the middle of their meal, when there is for them no chance of escape!'

He did his big laugh, and Sonja laughed too, though not so loudly. A power-cyclist, kitted out in what looked like a black wetsuit, went speeding by us, and for the next few moments, we all watched his frantic, receding shape.

'I went to Switzerland once,' I said eventually. 'A couple of summers ago. Interlaken. I stayed at the youth hostel there.'

'Ah yes, Interlaken. A beautiful place. Some Swiss people scoff at it. They say it is just for the tourists. But

Sonja and I always love to perform there. In fact, to play in Interlaken on a summer evening, to happy people from all over the world, it is something very wonderful. I hope you enjoyed your visit there.'

'Yeah, it was great.'

'There is a restaurant in Interlaken where we play a few nights every summer. For our performance, we position ourselves under the restaurant's canopy, so we are facing the dining tables, which of course are outdoors on such an evening. And as we perform, we are able to see all the tourists, eating and talking together under the stars. And behind the tourists, we see the big field, where during the day the paragliders are landing, but which at night is lit up by the lamps along the Höheweg. And if your eye may travel further, there are the Alps overlooking the field. The outlines of the Eiger, the Mönch, the Jungfrau. And the air is pleasantly warm and filled with the music we are making. I always feel when we are there, this is a privilege. I think, yes, it is good to be doing this.'

'That restaurant,' Sonja said. 'Last year, the manager made us wear full costumes while we performed, even though it was so hot. It was very uncomfortable, and we said, what difference does it make, why must we have our bulky waistcoats and scarves and hats? In just our blouses, we look neat and still very Swiss. But the restaurant manager tells us, we put on the full costumes or we don't play. Our choice, he says, and walks away, just like that.'

'But Sonja, that is the same in any job. There is always a uniform, something the employer insists you must wear. It is the same for bankers! And in our case, at least it is something we believe in. Swiss culture. Swiss tradition.'

Once again something vaguely awkward hovered between them, but it was just for a second or two, and then they both smiled as they fixed their gazes back on my guitar. I thought I should say something, so I said:

'I think I'd enjoy that. Being able to play in different countries. It must keep you sharp, really aware of your audiences.'

'Yes,' Tilo said, 'it is good that we perform to all kinds of people. And not only in Europe. All in all, we have got to know so many cities so well.'

'Düsseldorf, for instance,' said Sonja. There was something different about her voice now – something harder – and I could see again the person I'd encountered back at the cafe. Tilo, though, didn't seem to notice anything and said to me, in a carefree sort of way:

'Düsseldorf is where our son is now living. He is your age. Perhaps a little older.'

'Earlier this year,' Sonja said, 'we went to Düsseldorf. We have an engagement to play there. Not the usual thing, this is a chance to play our real music. So we call him, our son, our only child, we call to say we are coming to his city. He does not answer his phone, so we leave a message. We leave many messages. No reply. We arrive in Düsseldorf, we leave more messages. We say, here we are, we are in your city. Still nothing. Tilo says don't worry, perhaps he will come on the night, to our concert. But he does not come. We play, then we go to another city, to our next engagement.'

Tilo made a chuckling noise. 'I think perhaps Peter heard enough of our music while he was growing up! The poor boy, you see, he had to listen to us rehearsing, day after day.'

'I suppose it can be a bit tricky,' I said. 'Having children and being musicians.'

'We only had the one child,' Tilo said, 'so it was not so bad. Of course we were fortunate. When we had to travel, and we couldn't take him with us, his grandparents were always delighted to help. And when Peter was older, we were able to send him to a good boarding school. Again, his grandparents came to the rescue. We could not afford such school fees otherwise. So we were very fortunate.'

'Yes, we were fortunate,' Sonja said. 'Except Peter hated his school.'

The earlier good atmosphere was definitely slipping away. In an effort to cheer things up, I said quickly: 'Well, anyway, it looks like you both really enjoy your work.'

'Oh yes, we enjoy our work,' said Tilo. 'It's everything to us. Even so, we very much appreciate a vacation. Do you know, this is our first proper vacation in three years.'

This made me feel really bad all over again, and I thought about having another go at persuading them to change hotels, but I could see how ridiculous this would look. I just had to hope Hag Fraser pulled her finger out. Instead, I said:

'Look, if you like, I'll play you that song I was working on earlier. I haven't finished it, and I wouldn't usually do this. But since you heard some of it anyway, I don't mind playing you what I've got so far.'

The smile returned to Sonja's face. 'Yes,' she said, 'please do let us hear. It sounded so beautiful.'

As I got ready to play, they shifted again, so they were facing the view like before, their backs to me. But this time, instead of cuddling, they sat there on the grass with surprisingly upright postures, each with a hand up to the brow to shield away the sun. They stayed like that all the time I played, peculiarly still, and what with the way each of them cast a long afternoon shadow, they looked like matching art exhibits. I brought my incomplete song to a meandering halt, and for a moment they didn't move. Then their postures relaxed, and they applauded, though perhaps not quite as enthusiastically as the last time. Tilo got to his feet, muttering compliments, then helped Sonja up. It was only when you saw how they did this that you remembered they were really quite middle-aged. Maybe they were just tired. For all I know, they might have done a fair bit of walking before they'd come across me. All the same, it seemed to me they found it quite a struggle to get up.

'You've entertained us so marvellously,' Tilo was saying. 'Now we are the tourists, and someone else plays for us! It makes a pleasant change.'

'I would love to hear that song when it is finished,' Sonja said, and she seemed really to mean it. 'Maybe one day I will hear it on the radio. Who knows?'

'Yes,' Tilo said, 'and then Sonja and I will play our cover version to our customers!' His big laugh rang through the air. Then he did a polite little bow and said: 'So today we are in your debt three times over. A splendid lunch. A splendid choice of hotel. And a splendid concert here in the hills!'

As we said our goodbyes, I had an urge to tell them the truth. To confess that I'd deliberately sent them to the worst hotel in the area, and warn them to move out while there was still time. But the affectionate way they shook my hand made it all the harder to come out with this. And then they were going down the hill and I was alone on the bench again.

The cafe had closed by the time I came down from the hills. Maggie and Geoff looked exhausted. Maggie said it had been their busiest day yet and seemed pleased about it. But when Geoff made the same point over supper – which we ate in the cafe from various left-overs – he put it like it was a negative thing, like it was awful they'd been made to work so hard and where had I been to help? Maggie asked how my afternoon had gone, and I didn't mention Tilo and Sonja – that seemed too complicated – but told her I'd gone up to the Sugarloaf to work on my song. And when she asked if I'd made any progress, and I said yes, I was making real headway now, Geoff got up and marched out moodily, even though there was still food on his plate. Maggie pretended not to notice, and fair enough, he came back a few minutes later with a can of beer, and sat there reading his newspaper and not saying much. I didn't want to be the cause of a rift between my sister and brother-in-law, so I excused myself soon after that and went upstairs to work some more on the song.

My room, which was such an inspiration in the daytime, wasn't nearly so appealing after dark. For a start, the curtains didn't pull all the way across, which meant if I opened a window in the stifling heat, insects from miles around would see my light and come charging in. And the light I had was just this one bare bulb hanging down from the ceiling rose, which cast gloomy shadows all round the room, making it look all the more obviously the spare room it was. That evening, I was wanting light to work by, to jot down lyrics as they occurred to me. But it got far too stuffy, and in the end I switched off the bulb, pulled back the curtains, and opened the windows wide. Then I sat in the bay with my guitar, just the way I did in the day.

I'd been there like that for about an hour, playing through various ideas for the bridge passage, when there was a knock and Maggie stuck her head round the door. Of course everything was in darkness, but outside down on the terrace there was a security light, so I could just about make out her face. She had on this awkward smile, and I thought she was about to ask me to come and help with yet another chore. She came right in, closed the door behind her and said:

'I'm sorry, love. But Geoff's really tired tonight, he's been working so hard. And now he says he wants to watch his movie in peace?'

She said it like that, like it was a question, and it took me a moment to realise she was asking me to stop playing my music.

'But I'm working on something important here,' I said.

'I know. But he's really tired tonight, and he says he can't relax because of your guitar.'

'What Geoff needs to realise,' I said, 'is that just as he's got his work to do, I've got mine.'

My sister seemed to think about this. Then she did a big sigh. 'I don't think I ought to report that back to Geoff.'

'Why not? Why don't you? It's time he got the message.'

'Why not? Because I don't think he'd be very pleased, that's why not. And I don't really think he'd accept that his work and your work are quite on the same level.'

I stared at Maggie, for a moment quite speechless. Then I said: 'You're talking such rubbish. Why are you talking such rubbish?'

She shook her head wearily, but didn't say anything.

'I don't understand why you're talking such rubbish,' I said. 'And just when things are going so well for me.'

'Things are going well for you, are they, love?' She kept looking at me in the half-light. 'Well, all right,' she said in the end. 'I won't argue with you.' She turned away to open the door. 'Come down and join us, if you like,' she said as she left.

Rigid with rage, I stared at the door that had closed behind her. I became aware of muffled sounds from the television downstairs, and even in the state I was in, some detached part of my brain was telling me my fury should be directed not at Maggie, but at Geoff, who'd been systematically trying to undermine me ever since I'd got here. Even so, it was my sister I was livid at. In all the time I'd been in her house, she hadn't once asked to hear a song, the way Tilo and Sonja had done. Surely it wasn't too much to ask of your own sister, and one who'd been, I happened to remember, a big music fan in her teens? And now here she was, interrupting me when I was trying to work and talking all this rubbish. Every time I thought of the way she'd said: 'All right, I won't argue with you,' I felt fresh fury coursing through me.

I came down off the window sill, put away the guitar, and threw myself down on my mattress. Then for the next little while I stared at the patterns on the ceiling. It seemed clear I'd been invited here on false pretences, that this had all been about getting cheap help for the busy season, a mug they didn't even have to pay. And my sister didn't understand what I was trying to achieve any better than did her moron of a husband. It would serve them both right if I left them here in the lurch and went back to London. I kept going round and round with this stuff, until maybe an hour or so later, I calmed down a bit and decided I'd just turn in for the night.

I didn't speak much to either of them when I came down as usual just after the breakfast rush. I made some toast and coffee, helped myself to some left-over scrambled eggs, and settled down in the corner of the cafe. All through my breakfast the thought kept occurring to me I might run into Tilo and Sonja again up in the hills. And though this might mean having to face the music about Hag Fraser's place, even so, I realised I was hoping it would happen. Besides, even if Hag Fraser's was truly awful, they'd never suppose I'd recommended it out of malice. There'd be any number of ways for me to get out of it.

Maggie and Geoff were probably expecting me to help again with the lunch rush, but I decided they needed a lesson about taking people for granted. So after breakfast, I went upstairs, got my guitar and slipped out the back way.

It was really hot again and the sweat was running down my cheek as I climbed the path leading up to my bench. Even though I'd been thinking about Tilo and Sonja at breakfast, I'd forgotten them by this point, and so got a surprise when, coming up the final slope, I looked towards the bench and saw Sonja sitting there by herself. She spotted me immediately and waved.

I was still a bit wary of her, and especially without Tilo around, I wasn't so keen to sit down with her. But she gave me a big smile and did a shifting movement, like she was making room for me, so I didn't have much choice.

We said our hellos, then for a time we just sat there side by side, not speaking. This didn't seem so odd at first, partly because I was still getting my breath back, and partly because of the view. There was more haze and cloud than the previous day, but if you concentrated, you could still see beyond the Welsh borders to the Black Mountains. The breeze was quite strong, but not uncomfortable.

'So where's Tilo?' I asked in the end.

'Tilo? Oh . . .' She put her hand up to shield her eyes. Then she pointed. 'There. You see? Over there. That is Tilo.'

Some way in the distance, I could see a figure, in what might have been a green T-shirt and a white sun cap, moving along the rising path towards Worcestershire Beacon.

'Tilo wished to go for a walk,' she said.

'You didn't want to go with him?'

'No. I decided to stay here.'

While she wasn't by any means the irate customer from the cafe, neither was she quite the same person who'd been so warm and encouraging to me the day before. There was definitely something up, and I started preparing my defence about Hag Fraser's.

'By the way,' I said, 'I've been working a bit more on that song. You can hear it if you like.'

She gave this consideration, then said: 'If you do not mind, perhaps not just at this minute. You see, Tilo and I have just had a talk. You might call it a disagreement.'

'Oh okay. Sorry to hear that.'

'And now he has gone off for his walk.'

Again, we sat there not talking. Then I sighed and said: 'I think maybe this is all my fault.'

She turned to look at me. 'Your fault? Why do you say that?'

'The reason you've quarrelled, the reason your holiday's all messed up now. It's my fault. It's that hotel, isn't it? It wasn't very good, right?'

'The hotel?' She seemed puzzled. 'That hotel. Well, it has some weak points. But it is a hotel, like many others.'

'But you noticed, right? You noticed all the weak points. You must have done.'

She seemed to think this over, then nodded. 'It is true, I noticed the weak points. Tilo, however, did not. Tilo, of course, thought the hotel was splendid. We are so lucky, he kept saying. So lucky to find such a hotel. Then this morning we have our breakfast. For Tilo, this is a fine breakfast, the best breakfast ever. I say, Tilo, don't be stupid. This is not a good breakfast. This is not a good hotel. He says, no, no, we are so very lucky. So I become angry. I tell the proprietress everything that is wrong. Tilo leads me away.

Let's go for a walk, he says. You will feel better then. So we come out here. And he says, Sonja, look at these hills, aren't they so beautiful? Aren't we fortunate to come to such a place as this for our vacation? These hills, he says, are even more wonderful than he imagined them when we listen to Elgar. He asks me, isn't this so? Perhaps I become angry again. I tell him, these hills are not so wonderful. It is not how I imagine them when I hear Elgar's music. Elgar's hills are majestic and mysterious. Here, this is just like a park. This is what I say to him, and then it is his turn to be cross. He says in that case, he will walk by himself. He says we are finished, we never agree on anything now. Yes, he says, Sonja, you and me, we are finished. And off he goes! So there you are. That is why he is up there and I am down here.' She shielded her eyes again and watched Tilo's progress.

'I'm really sorry,' I said. 'If only I hadn't sent you to that hotel in the first place . . .'

'Please. The hotel is not important.' She leaned forward to get a better view of Tilo. Then she turned to me and smiled, and I thought maybe there were little tears in her eyes. 'Tell me,' she said. 'Today, you mean to write more songs?'

'That's the plan. Or at least, I want to finish the one I've been working on. The one you heard yesterday.'

'That was beautiful. And what will you do then, once you have finished writing your songs here? You have a plan?'

'I'll go back to London and form a band. These songs need just the right band or they won't work.'

'How exciting. I do wish you luck.'

After a moment, I said, quite quietly: 'Then again, I may not bother. It's not so easy, you know.'

She didn't reply, and it occurred to me she hadn't heard, because she'd turned away again, to look towards Tilo.

'You know,' she said eventually, 'when I was younger, nothing could make me angry. But now I get angry at many things. I don't know how I have become this way. It is not good. Well, I do not think Tilo is coming back here. I will return to the hotel and wait for him.' She got to her feet, her gaze still fixed on his distant figure.

'It's a shame,' I said, also getting up, 'you having a row on your holiday. And yesterday, when I was playing to you, you seemed so happy together.'

'Yes, that was a good moment. Thank you for that.' Suddenly, she held out her hand to me, smiling warmly. 'It has been so nice to meet you.'

We shook hands, in the slightly limp way you do with women. She started to walk away, then stopped and looked at me.

'If Tilo were here,' she said, 'he would say to you, never be discouraged. He would say, of course, you must go to London and try and form your band. Of course you will be successful. That is what Tilo would say to you. Because that is his way.'

'And what would *you* say?'

'I would like to say the same. Because you are young and talented. But I am not so certain. As it is, life will bring enough disappointments. If on top, you have such dreams as this . . .' She smiled again and shrugged. 'But I should not say these things. I am not a good example to you. Besides, I can see you are much more like Tilo. If disappointments do come, you will carry on still. You will say, just as he does, I am so lucky.' For a few seconds, she went on gazing at me, like she was memorising the way I looked. The breeze was blowing her hair about, making her seem older than she usually did. 'I wish you much luck,' she said finally.

'Good luck yourself,' I said. 'And I hope you two make it up okay.'

She waved a last time, then went off down the path out of my view.

I took the guitar from its case and sat back on the bench. I didn't play anything for a while though, because I was looking into the distance, towards Worcestershire Beacon, and Tilo's tiny figure up on the incline. Maybe it was to do with the way the sun was hitting that part of the hill, but I could see him much more clearly now than before, even though he'd got further away. He'd paused for a moment on the path, and seemed to be looking about him at the surrounding hills, almost like he was trying to reappraise them. Then his figure started to move again.

I worked on my song for a few minutes, but kept losing concentration, mainly because I was thinking about the way Hag Fraser's face must have looked as Sonja laid into her that morning. Then I gazed at the clouds, and at the sweep of land below me, and I made myself think again about my song, and the bridge passage I still hadn't got right.

[123]

Nocturne

UNTIL TWO DAYS AGO, Lindy Gardner was my next-door neighbor. Okay, you're thinking, if Lindy Gardner was my neighbor, that probably means I live in Beverly Hills; a movie producer, maybe, or an actor or a musician. Well, I'm a musician all right. But though I've played behind one or two performers you'll have heard of, I'm not what you'd call big-league. My manager, Bradley Stevenson, who in his way has been a good friend over the years, maintains I have it in me to be big-league. Not just big-league session player, but big-league headliner. It's not true saxophonists don't become headliners any more, he says, and repeats his list of names. Marcus Lightfoot. Silvio Tarrentini. They're all jazz players, I point out. 'What are you, if you're not a jazz player?' he says. But only in my innermost dreams am I still a jazz player. In the real world – when I don't have my face entirely wrapped in bandages the way I do now – I'm just a jobbing tenor man, in reasonable demand for studio work, or when a band's lost their regular guy. If it's pop they want, it's pop I play. R&B? Fine. Car commercials, the walk-on theme for a talk show, I'll do it. I'm a jazz player these days only when I'm inside my cubicle.

I'd prefer to play in my living room, but our apartment's so cheaply made the neighbors would start complaining all the way down the hall. So what I've done is convert our smallest room into a rehearsal room. It's no more than a closet really – you can get an office chair in there and that's it – but I've sound-proofed it with foam and egg-trays and old padded envelopes my manager Bradley sent round from his office. Helen, my wife, when she used to live with me, she'd see me going in there with my sax and she'd laugh and say it was like I was going to the toilet, and sometimes that's how it felt. That's to say, it was like I was sitting in that dim, airless cubicle taking care of personal business no one else would ever care to come across.

You've guessed by now Lindy Gardner never lived next to this apartment I'm talking about. Neither was she one of the neighbors who banged the door whenever I played out-side the cubicle. When I said she was my neighbor, I meant something else, and I'm going to explain this right now.

Until two days ago, Lindy was in the next room here at this swanky hotel, and like me, had her face encased in bandages. Lindy, of course, has a big comfortable house nearby, and hired help, so Dr Boris let her go home. In fact, from a strictly medical viewpoint, she could probably have gone much sooner, but there were clearly other fac-tors. For one, it wouldn't be so easy for her to hide from cameras and gossip columnists back in her own house. What's more, my hunch is Dr Boris's stellar reputation is based on procedures that aren't one hundred per cent legal, and that's why he hides his patients up here on this hush-hush floor of the hotel, cut off from all regular staff and guests, with instructions to leave our rooms only when absolutely necessary. If you could see past all the crêpe, you'd spot more stars up here in a week than in a month at the Chateau Marmont.

So how does someone like me get to be here among these stars and millionaires, having my face altered by the top man in town? I guess it started with my manager, Bradley, who isn't so big-league himself, and doesn't look any more like George Clooney than I do. He first mentioned it a few years ago, in a jokey sort of way, then seemed to get more serious each time he brought it up again. What he was saying, in a nutshell, was that I was ugly. And that this was what was keeping me from the big league.

'Look at Marcus Lightfoot,' he said. 'Look at Kris Bugoski. Or Tarrentini. Do any of them have a signature sound the way you do? No. Do they have your tenderness? Your vision? Do they have even half your technique? No. But they look right, so doors keep opening for them.'

'What about Billy Fogel?' I said. 'He's ugly as hell and he's doing fine.'

'Billy's ugly all right. But he's sexy, bad guy ugly. You, Steve, you're . . . Well, you're dull, loser ugly. The wrong kind of ugly. Listen, have you ever considered having a little work done? Of a surgical nature, I mean?'

I went home and repeated this all to Helen because I thought she'd find it as funny as I did. And at first, sure enough, we had a lot of laughs at Bradley's expense. Then Helen came over, put her arms around me and told me that for her at least, I was the most handsome guy in the universe. Then she kind of took a step back and went quiet, and when

I asked her what was wrong, she said nothing was wrong.
Then she said that perhaps, just perhaps, Bradley had a
point. Maybe I *should* consider having a little work done.

'No need to look at me like that!' she yelled back.
'Everyone's doing it. And you, you have a *professional* reason. Guy wants to be a fancy chauffeur, he goes and buys a
fancy car. It's no different with you!'

But at that stage I gave the idea no further thought,
even if I was beginning to accept this notion that I was
'loser ugly'. For one thing, I didn't have the money. In fact,
the very moment Helen was talking about fancy chauf-
feurs, we were nine and a half thousand dollars in debt.
This was characteristic of Helen. A fine person in many
ways, but this ability to forget completely the true state of
our finances and start dreaming up major new spending
opportunities, this was very Helen.

Money aside, I didn't like the idea of someone cutting
me up. I'm not so good with that kind of thing. One time,
early in my relationship with Helen, she invited me to go
running with her. It was a crisp winter's morning, and I've
never been much of a jogger, but I was taken by her and
anxious to impress. So there we were running around the
park, and I was doing fine keeping up with her, when suddenly my shoe hit something very hard jutting out of the
ground. I could feel a pain in my foot, which wasn't so bad,
but when I took off my sneaker and sock, and saw the nail
on my big toe rearing up from the flesh like it was doing a
Hitler-style salute, I got nauseous and fainted. That's the
way I am. So you can see, I wasn't wild about face surgery.

Then, naturally, there was the principle of the thing.

Okay, I've told you before, I'm no stickler for artistic integrity. I play every kind of bubble-gum for the pay. But this proposition was of another order, and I did have some pride left. Bradley was right about one thing: I was twice as talented as most other people in this town. But it seemed that didn't count for much these days. Because it has to do with image, marketability, being in magazines and on TV shows, about parties and who you ate lunch with. It all made me sick. I was a musician, why should I have to join in this game? Why couldn't I just play my music the best way I knew, and keep getting better, if only in my cubicle, and maybe some day, just maybe, genuine music lovers would hear me and appreciate what I was doing. What did I want with a plastic surgeon?

At first Helen seemed to see it my way, and the topic didn't come up again for some time. That is, not until she phoned from Seattle to say she was leaving me and moving in with Chris Prendergast, a guy she'd known since high school and who now owned a string of successful diners across Washington. I'd met this Prendergast a few times over the years – he'd even come to dinner once – but I'd never suspected a thing. 'All that sound-proofing in that cupboard of yours,' Bradley said at the time. 'It works both ways.' I suppose he had a point.

But I don't want to dwell on Helen and Prendergast except to explain their part in getting me where I am now. Maybe you're thinking I drove up the coast, confronted the happy couple, and plastic surgery became necessary following a manly altercation with my rival. Romantic, but no, that's not the way it happened.

What happened was that a few weeks after her phone call, Helen came back to the apartment to organise moving out her belongings. She looked sad walking around the place – where, after all, we'd had some happy times. I kept thinking she was about to cry, but she didn't, and just went on putting all her things into neat piles. Someone would be along to pick them up in a day or two, she said. Then as I was on my way to my cubicle, tenor in hand, she looked up and said quietly:

'Steve, please. Don't go into that place again. We need to talk.'

'Talk about what?'

'Steve, for God's sake.'

So I put the sax back in its case and we went into our little kitchen and sat down at the table facing one another. Then she put it to me.

There was no going back on her decision. She was happy with Prendergast, for whom she'd carried a torch since school. But she felt bad about leaving me, especially at a time when my career wasn't going so good. So she'd thought things over and talked with her new guy, and he too had felt bad about me. Apparently, what he'd said was: 'It's just too bad Steve has to pay the price for all our happiness.' So here was the deal. Prendergast was willing to pay for me to have my face fixed by the best surgeon in town. 'It's true,' she said, when I looked back at her blankly. 'He means it. No expense spared. All the hospital bills, recuperation, everything. The best surgeon in town.' Once my face was fixed, there'd be nothing holding me back, she said. I'd go right to the top, how could I fail, with the kind of talent I had?

'Steve, why are you looking at me like that? This is a great offer. And God knows if he'll still be willing in six months. Say yes right now and do yourself a big favor. It's just a few weeks of discomfort, then whoosh! Jupiter and beyond!'

Fifteen minutes later, on her way out, she said in much sterner tones: 'So what is it you're saying? That you're happy playing in that little closet for the rest of your life? That you just love being this big a loser?' And with that, she left.

The next day I went into Bradley's office to see if he had anything for me, and I happened to mention what had occurred, expecting us to laugh about it. But he didn't laugh at all.

'This guy's rich? And he's willing to get you a top surgeon? Maybe he'll get you Crespo. Or even Boris.'

So now I had Bradley too, telling me how I had to take this opportunity, how if I didn't I'd be a loser all my life. I left his office pretty angry, but he phoned later that same afternoon and kept on about it. If it was the call itself holding me back, he said, if it was the blow to my pride involved in picking up a phone and saying to Helen, yes, please, I want to do it, please get your boyfriend to sign that big check, if that's what was holding me up, then he, Bradley, was happy to do all the negotiations on my behalf. I told him to go sit on a tall spike, and hung up. But then he called again an hour later. He told me he'd now figured it all out and I was a fool not to have done so myself.

'Helen's got this carefully planned. Consider her position. She loves you. But looks-wise, well, you're an embarrassment when you're seen in public. You're no turn-on. She wants you to do something about it, but you refuse. So what's she to do? Well, her next move's magnificent. Full of subtlety. As a professional manager I have to admire it. She goes off with this guy. Okay, maybe she's always had the hots for him, but really, she doesn't love him at all. She gets the guy to pay for your face. Once you're healed up, she comes back, you're good-looking, she's hungry for your body, she can't wait to be seen with you in restaurants . . .'

I stopped him here to point out that though over the years I'd become accustomed to the depths to which he could sink when persuading me to do something to his professional advantage, this latest ploy was somewhere so far down in the pits it was a place no light penetrated and where steaming horseshit would freeze in seconds. And on the subject of horseshit, I told him that while I understood how he, on account of his nature, couldn't help shoveling the stuff all the time, it would still be sound strategy on his part to come up with the sort that had at least a chance of taking me in for a minute or two. Then I hung up on him again.

Over the next few weeks, work seemed scarcer than ever, and each time I called Bradley to see if he had anything, he'd say something like: 'It's hard to help a guy who won't help himself.' In the end, I began considering the whole matter more pragmatically. I couldn't get away from the fact that I needed to eat. And if going through with this meant that eventually a lot more people got to hear my music, was that such a bad result? And what about my plans to lead my own band one day? How was that ever going to happen?

Finally, maybe six weeks after Helen came up with the offer, I mentioned casually to Bradley that I was thinking it over again. That was all he needed. He was off, making phone calls and arrangements, shouting a lot and getting excited. To give him his due, he was true to his word: he did all the go-between stuff so I didn't have to have a single humiliating conversation with Helen, let alone with Prendergast. At times Bradley even managed to create the illusion he was negotiating a deal for me, that it was me who had something to sell. Even so, I was having doubts several times each day. When it happened, it happened suddenly. Bradley called to say Dr Boris had a last-minute cancellation and I had to get myself to a particular address by three-thirty that same afternoon with all my bags packed. Maybe I had some final jitters at that point, because I remember Bradley yelling down the phone at me to pull myself together, that he was coming to get me himself, and then I was being driven up winding roads to a big house in the Hollywood hills and put under anesthetic, just like a character in a Raymond Chandler story.

After a couple of days I was brought down here, to this Beverly Hills hotel, by the back entrance under cover of dark, and wheeled down this corridor, so exclusive we're sealed off entirely from all the regular life of the hotel.

The first week, my face was painful and the anesthetic in my system made me nauseous. I had to sleep propped up on pillows, which meant I didn't sleep much at all, and because my nurse insisted on keeping the room dark all the time, I lost sense of what hour of the day it was. Even so, I

didn't feel at all bad. In fact, I felt exhilarated and opti-
mistic. I felt complete confidence in Dr Boris, who was
after all a guy in whose hands movie stars placed their
entire careers. What's more, I knew that with me he'd
completed his masterpiece; that on seeing my loser's face,
he'd felt his deepest ambitions stir, remembered why he'd
chosen his vocation in the first place, and put everything
into it and more. When the bandages came off, I could
look forward to a cleanly chiseled face, slightly brutal, yet
full of nuance. A guy with his reputation, after all, would
have thought through carefully the requirements of a serious jazz musician, and not confused them with, say, those
of a TV anchorman. He may even have put in something
to give me that vaguely haunted quality, kind of like the
young De Niro, or like Chet Baker before the drugs rav-
aged him. I thought about the albums I'd make, the
line-ups I'd hire to back me. I felt triumphant and couldn't
believe I'd ever hesitated about the move.

Then came the second week, when the effect of the
drugs wore off, and I felt depressed, lonely and cheap. My
nurse, Gracie, now let a little more light into the room –
though she kept the blinds at least halfway down – and I
was allowed to walk about the room in my dressing gown.
So I put one CD after another into the Bang & Olufsen
and went round and round the carpet, now and then stop-
ping in front of the dressing-table mirror to inspect the
weird bandaged monster gazing back through peephole
eyes.

It was during this phase that Gracie first told me Lindy
Gardner was next door. Had she brought this news in my

earlier, euphoric phase, I'd have greeted it with delight. I
might even have taken it as the first indicator of the glamorous life I was now headed for. Coming when it did
though, just as I was falling into my trough, the news filled
me with such disgust it set off another bout of nausea. If
you're one of Lindy's many admirers, I apologise for what's
coming up here. But the fact was, at that moment, if there
was one figure who epitomised for me everything that was
shallow and sickening about the world, it was Lindy
Gardner: a person with negligible talent – okay, let's face it,
she's *demonstrated* she can't act, and she doesn't even pretend to have musical ability – but who's managed all the
same to become famous, fought over by TV networks and
glossy magazines who can't get enough of her smiling features. I went past a bookstore earlier this year and saw a
snaking line and wondered if someone like Stephen King
was around, and here it turns out to be Lindy signing
copies of her latest ghosted autobiography. And how was
this all achieved? The usual way, of course. The right love
affairs, the right marriages, the right divorces. All leading
to the right magazine covers, the right talk shows, then
stuff like that recent thing she had on the air, I don't
remember its name, where she gave advice about how to
dress for that first big date after your divorce, or what to do
if you suspect your husband is gay, all of that. You hear
people talk about her 'star quality', but the spell's easy
enough to analyse. It's the sheer accumulation of TV
appearances and glossy covers, of all the photos you've seen
of her at premieres and parties, her arm linked to legendary
people. And now here she was, right next door, recovering

just like me from a face job by Dr Boris. No other news could have symbolised more perfectly the scale of my moral descent. The week before, I'd been a jazz musician. Now I was just another pathetic hustler, getting my face fixed in a bid to crawl after the Lindy Gardners of this world into vacuous celebrity.

The next few days, I tried to pass the time reading, but couldn't concentrate. Under the bandages, parts of my face throbbed awfully, others itched like hell and I had bouts of feeling hot and claustrophobic. I longed to play my sax, and the thought that it would be weeks yet until I could put my facial muscles under that kind of pressure made me even more despondent. In the end, I worked out the best way to get through the day was to alternate listening to CDs with spells of staring at sheet music – I'd brought the folder of charts and lead sheets I worked with in my cubicle – and humming improvisations to myself.

It was towards the end of the second week, when I was starting to feel a little better both physically and mentally, my nurse handed me an envelope with a knowing smile, saying: 'Now that ain't something you'll get every day.' Inside was a page of hotel notepaper, and since I've got it right here beside me, I'll quote it just the way it came.

Gracie tells me you're getting weary of this high life. I'm that way too. How about you come and visit? If five o'clock tonight isn't too early for cocktails? Dr B. says no alcohol, I expect same for you. So looks like club sodas and Perrier. Curse him! See you at five or I'll be heartbroken. Lindy Gardner.

Maybe it was because I'd become so bored by this point; or just that my mood was on the up again; or that the thought of having a fellow prisoner to swap stories with was extremely appealing. Or maybe I wasn't so immune myself to the glamor thing. In any case, despite everything I felt about Lindy Gardner, when I read this, I felt a tingle of excitement, and I found myself telling Gracie to let Lindy know I'd be over at five.

Lindy Gardner had on even more bandages than I did. I'd at least been left an opening at the top, from which my hair sprang up like palms in a desert oasis. But Boris had encased the whole of Lindy's head so it was a contoured coconut shape, with slots only for eyes, nose and mouth. What had happened to all that luxuriant blonde hair, I didn't know. Her voice, though, wasn't as constricted as you'd expect, and I recognised it from the times I'd seen her on TV.

'So how are you finding all this?' she asked. When I replied I wasn't finding it too bad, she said: 'Steve. May I call you Steve? I've heard all about you from Gracie.'

'Oh? I hope she left out the bad part.'

'Well, I know you're a musician. And a very promising one too.'

'She told you that?'

'Steve, you're tense. I want you to relax when you're with me. Some famous people, I know, they *like* the public to be tense around them. Makes them feel all the more special. But I hate that. I want you to treat me just like I'm one of your regular friends. What were you telling me? You were saying you don't mind this so much.'

Her room was significantly bigger than mine, and this was just the lounge part of her suite. We were sitting facing each other on matching white sofas, and between us was a low coffee table made of smoked glass, through which I could see the hunk of driftwood it rested on. Its surface was covered with shiny magazines and a fruit basket still in cellophane. Like me, she had the air-conditioning up high – it gets warm in bandages – and the blinds low over the windows against the evening sun. A maid had just brought me a glass of water and a coffee, both with straws bobbing in them – which is how everything has to be served here – then had left the room.

In answer to her question, I told her the toughest part for me was not being able to play my sax.

'But you can see why Boris won't let you,' she said. 'Just imagine. You blow on that horn a day before you're ready, bits of your face will fly out all over the room!'

She seemed to find this pretty funny, waving her hand at me, as though it was me that had made the wisecrack and she was saying: 'Stop it, you're too much!' I laughed with her, and sipped some coffee through the straw. Then she began talking about various friends who'd recently gone through cosmetic surgery, what they'd reported, funny things that had happened to them. Every person she mentioned was a celebrity or else married to one.

'So you're a sax player,' she said, suddenly changing the subject. 'You made a good choice. It's a wonderful instrument. You know what I say to all young saxophone players? I tell them to listen to the old pros. I knew this sax player, up-and-coming like you, only ever listened to these far-out

guys. Wayne Shorter and people like that. I said to him,
you'll learn more from the old pros. Might not have been
so ground-breaking, I said to him, but those old pros knew
how to do it. Steve, do you mind if I play you something?
To show you exactly what I'm talking about?'

'No, I don't mind. But Mrs Gardner . . .'

'Please. Call me Lindy. We're equals here.'

'Okay. Lindy. I just wanted to say, I'm not so young. In
fact, I'll be thirty-nine next birthday.'

'Oh really? Well, that's still young. But you're right, I
thought you were much younger. With these exclusive
masks Boris has given us, it's hard to tell, right? From what
Gracie said, I thought you were this up-and-coming kid,
and maybe your parents had paid for this surgery to get
you off to a flying start. Sorry, my mistake.'

'Gracie said I was "up-and-coming"?'

'Don't be hard on her. She said you were a musician so I
asked her your name. And when I said I wasn't familiar
with it, she said, "That's because he's up-and-coming."
That's all it was. Hey, but listen, what does it matter how
old you are? You can always learn from the old pros. I want
you to listen to this. I think you'll find it interesting.'

She went over to a cabinet and a moment later held up
a CD. 'You'll appreciate this. The sax on this is so perfect.'

Her room had a Bang & Olufsen system just like mine,
and soon the place filled with lush strings. A few measures
in, a sleepy, Ben Webster-ish tenor broke through and pro-
ceeded to lead the orchestra. If you didn't know too much
about these things, you could even have mistaken it for one
of those Nelson Riddle intros for Sinatra. But the voice

that eventually came on belonged to Tony Gardner. The song – I just about remembered it – was something called "Back at Culver City", a ballad that never quite made it and which no one plays much any more. All the time Tony Gardner sang, the sax kept up with him, replying to him line by line. The whole thing was utterly predictable, and way too sugary.

After a while, though, I'd stopped paying much attention to the music because there was Lindy in front of me, gone into a kind of dream, dancing slowly to the song. Her movements were easy and graceful – clearly the surgery hadn't extended to her body – and she had a shapely, slim figure. She was wearing something that was part night-gown, part cocktail dress; that's to say, it was at the same time vaguely medical yet glamorous. Also, I was trying to work something out. I'd had the distinct impression Lindy had recently divorced Tony Gardner, but given I'm the nation's worst when it comes to showbiz gossip, I began to think maybe I'd got it wrong. Otherwise why was she dancing this way, lost in the music, evidently enjoying herself?

Tony Gardner stopped singing a moment, the strings swelled into the bridge, and the piano player started a solo. At this point, Lindy seemed to come back to the planet. She stopped swaying around, turned the music off with the remote, then came and sat down in front of me.

'Isn't that marvelous? You see what I mean?'

'Yeah, that was beautiful,' I said, not sure whether we were still only talking about the sax.

'Your ears weren't deceiving you, by the way.'

'I'm sorry?'

'The singer. That was who you thought it was. Just because he's no longer my husband, that doesn't mean I can't play his records, right?'

'No, of course not.'

'And that's a lovely saxophone. You see now why I wanted you to hear it.'

'Yeah, it was beautiful.'

'Steve, are there recordings of you somewhere? I mean, of your own playing?'

'Sure. In fact I have a few CDs with me next door.'

'The next time you come, sweetie, I want you to bring them. I want to hear how you sound. Will you do that?'

'Okay, if it's not going to bore you.'

'Oh no, it won't bore me. But I hope you don't think I'm nosy. Tony always used to say I was nosy, I should just let people be, but you know, I think he was just being snobby. A lot of famous people, they think they should be interested only in other famous people. I've never been that way. I see everybody as a potential friend. Take Gracie. She's my friend. All my staff at home, they're also my friends. You should see me at parties. Everyone else, they're talking to each other about their latest movie or whatever, I'm the one having a conversation with the catering girl or the bartender. I don't think that's being nosy, do you?'

'No, I don't think that's nosy at all. But look, Mrs Gardner . . .'

'Lindy, please.'

'Lindy. Look, it's been fabulous being with you. But these drugs, they really tire me out. I think I'm going to have to go lie down for a while.'

'Oh, you're not feeling well?'

'It's nothing. It's just these drugs.'

'Too bad! You definitely have to come back when you're feeling better. And bring those recordings, the ones with you playing. Is that a deal?'

I had to reassure her some more that I'd had a good time and that I'd come back. Then as I was going out the door, she said:

'Steve, do you play chess? I'm the world's worst chess player, but I've got the cutest chess set. Meg Ryan brought it in for me last week.'

Back in my own room, I took a Coke from the mini-bar, sat down at the writing desk and looked out my window. There was a big pink sunset now, we were a long way up, and I could see the cars moving along the freeway in the distance. After a few minutes I phoned Bradley, and though his secretary kept me on hold a long time, he eventually came on the line.

'How's the face?' he asked worriedly, like he was inquiring after a well-loved pet he'd left in my care.

'How should I know? I'm still the Invisible Man.'

'Are you all right? You sound . . . dispirited.'

'I *am* dispirited. This whole thing was a mistake. I can see that now. It's not going to work.'

There was a moment's silence, then he asked: 'The operation's a failure?'

'I'm sure the operation's fine. I mean all the rest of it, what it's going to lead to. This *scheme* . . . It's never going to play out the way you said. I should never have let you talk me into it.'

'What's the matter with you? You sound depressed. What have they been pumping into you?'

'I'm fine. In fact, my head's straighter than it's been for a long while. That's the trouble. I can see it now. Your scheme . . . I should never have listened to you.'

'What is this? What scheme? Look, Steve, this isn't complicated. You're a very talented artist. When you're through with this, all you do is what you've always done. Just now you're simply removing an obstacle, that's all. There's no *scheme* . . .'

'Look, Bradley, it's bad here. It's not just the physical discomfort. I realise now what I'm doing to myself. It's been a mistake, I should have had more respect for myself.'

'Steve, what's triggered this? Did something just happen over there?'

'Damn right something happened. That's why I'm calling, I need you to get me out of this. I need you to get me to a different hotel.'

'Different hotel? Who are you? Crown Prince Abdullah? What the fuck's wrong with the hotel?'

'What's wrong is I've got Lindy Gardner right next door. And she just invited me over, and she's going to keep on inviting me over. That's what's wrong!'

'Lindy Gardner's next door?'

'Look, I can't go through that again. I've just been in there, it was all I could do to stay as long as I did. And now she's saying we have to play with her Meg Ryan chess set . . .'

'Steve, you're telling me Lindy Gardner's next door? You spent time with her?'

'She put on her husband's record! Fuck it, I think she's playing another one right now. This is what I've come to. This is my level now.'

'Steve, hold it, let's go over this again. Steve, just shut the fuck up, then explain it to me. Explain to me how you get to be with Lindy Gardner.'

I did calm down then for a while, and I gave a brief account of how Lindy had asked me over, and the way things had gone.

'So you weren't rude to her?' he asked as soon as I was through.

'No, I wasn't rude to her. I kept it all held in. But I'm not going back in there. I need to change hotels.'

'Steve, you're not going to change hotels. Lindy Gardner? She's in bandages, you're in bandages. She's right next door. Steve, this is a golden opportunity.'

'It's nothing of the sort, Bradley. It's inner-circle hell. Her Meg Ryan chess set for God's sake!'

'Meg Ryan chess set? How does that work? Every piece looks like Meg?'

'And she wants to hear my playing! She's insisting next time I take in CDs!'

'She wants to . . . Jesus, Steve, you haven't even got the bandages off and everything's going your way. She wants to hear you play?'

'I'm asking you to deal with this, Bradley. Okay, I'm in deep, I've had the surgery, you talked me into it, because I was fool enough to believe what you said. But I don't have to put up with this. I don't have to spend the next two weeks with Lindy Gardner. I'm asking you to get me moved pronto!'

'I'm not getting you moved anywhere. Do you realise how important a person Lindy Gardner is? You know the kind of people she's pals with? What she could do for you with one phone call? Okay, she's divorced from Tony Gardner now. That doesn't change a thing. Get her on your team, get your new face, doors will open. It'll be big league, five seconds flat.'

'It won't be big-league anything, Bradley, because I'm not going over there again, and I don't want any doors opening for me other than ones that open because of my music. And I don't believe what you said before, I don't believe this crap about a scheme . . .'

'I don't think you should be expressing yourself so emphatically. I'm very concerned about those stitches . . .'

'Bradley, very soon you won't have to be concerned about my stitches at all, because you know what? I'm going to pull off this mummy mask and I'm going to put my fingers into the corners of my mouth and yank my face into every kind of stretchy combination possible! Do you hear me, Bradley?'

I heard him sigh. Then he said: 'Okay, calm down. Just calm down. You've been under a lot of stress lately. It's understandable. If you don't want to see Lindy right now, if you want to let gold go floating by, okay, I understand your position. But be polite, okay? Make a good excuse. Don't burn any bridges.'

*

I felt a lot better after this talk with Bradley, and had a rea-
sonably contented evening, watching half a movie, then
listening to Bill Evans. The next morning after breakfast,
Dr Boris came in with two nurses, seemed satisfied and
left. A little later, around eleven, I had a visitor – a drum-
mer called Lee who I'd played with in a house band in San
Diego a few years ago. Bradley, who's also Lee's manager,
had suggested he come by.

Lee's okay and I was pleased to see him. He stayed for
an hour or so, and we swapped news of mutual friends,
who was in which band, who'd packed their bags and gone
to Canada or to Europe.

'It's too bad how so many of the old team aren't around
any more,' he said. 'You have great times together, next
thing you don't know where they are.'

He told me about his recent gigs, and we laughed over
some memories from our San Diego days. Then towards
the end of his visit, he said:

'And what about Jake Marvell? What do you make of it?
Strange world, ain't it?'

'It's strange all right,' I said. 'But then again, Jake was
always a good musician. He deserves what he's getting.'

'Yeah, but it's strange. Remember how Jake was back
then? In San Diego? Steve, you could have blown him off
the stage every night of the week. And now look at him. Is
that just luck or what?'

'Jake was always a nice guy,' I said. 'And as far as I'm concerned, it's good to see any sax player getting recognition.'

'Recognition's right,' Lee said. 'And right here in this
hotel too. Let me see, I've got it here.' He rummaged in his

bag and produced a tattered copy of *LA Weekly*. 'Yeah, here it is. The Simon and Wesbury Music Awards. Jazz Musician of the Year. Jake Marvell. Let's see, when is this fucker? Tomorrow down in the ballroom. You could take a stroll down those stairs and attend the ceremony.' He put down the paper and shook his head. 'Jake Marvell. Jazz Musician of the Year. Who'd have thought it, eh, Steve?'

'I guess I won't make it downstairs,' I said. 'But I'll remember to raise a glass to him.'

'Jake Marvell. Boy, is this a screwed-up world or what?'

About an hour after lunch, the phone rang and it was Lindy.

'The chess set's all laid out, sweetie,' she said. 'You ready to play? Don't say no, I'm going crazy here with boredom. Oh, and don't forget now, bring those CDs. I'm just dying to hear your playing.'

I put down the phone, then sat on the edge of the bed trying to figure out how it was I hadn't stood my ground better. In fact, I hadn't put up even a hint of a 'no'. Maybe it was plain spinelessness. Or maybe I'd taken on board much more of Bradley's argument on the phone than I'd admitted. But now there wasn't time to think about it, because I had to decide which of my CDs were most likely to impress her. The more avant-garde stuff was definitely out, as was the stuff I'd recorded with the electro-funk guys in San Francisco last year. In the end, I chose just the one CD, changed into a fresh shirt, put my dressing gown back over the top and went next door.

*

She too had on a dressing gown, but it was the kind she could have worn to a movie premiere without too much embarrassment. Sure enough, the chess set was there on the low glass table, and we sat down on opposite sides like before and began a game. Maybe because we had something to do with our hands, things felt much more relaxed than the last time. As we played, we found ourselves talking about this and that: TV shows, her favourite European cities, Chinese food. There was far less name-dropping this time round, and she seemed much calmer. At one point she said:

'You know what I do to stop myself going crazy in this place? My big secret? I'll tell you, but not a word, not even to Gracie, promise? What I do is go out for midnight walks. Just inside this building, but it's so vast you can walk around forever. And in the dead of night, it's amazing. Last night I was out there maybe a whole hour? You have to be careful, there's still staff roving around all the time, but I've never been caught. I hear anything at all, I run away and hide somewhere. Once these cleaning guys saw me for a second, but like *that* I was away into the shadows! It's so exciting. All day you're this prisoner, then it's like you're completely free, it's truly wonderful. I'm gonna take you with me some night, sweetie. I'll show you great things. The bars, the restaurants, conference rooms. Wonderful ballroom. And there's no one there, everything's just dark and empty. And I discovered the most fantastic place, a kind of penthouse, I think it's gonna be a presidential suite? They're halfway through building it, but I found it and I was able to walk right in, and I stayed there, twenty minutes, half an hour, just thinking things over. Hey,

Steve, is this right? I can do this and take your queen?'

'Oh. Yeah, I guess so. I didn't see that. Hey, Lindy, you're a lot smarter at this than you let on. Now what am I supposed to do?'

'All right, I tell you what. Since you're the guest, and you were obviously distracted by what I was saying, I'm gonna pretend I never saw it. Isn't that nice of me? Say, Steve, I can't remember if I asked you this before. You're married, right?'

'That's right.'

'So what does she think of all this? I mean, this isn't cheap. Quite a few pairs of shoes she could buy with this kind of money.'

'She's okay about it. In fact, this was her idea in the first place. Look who's not paying attention now.'

'Oh hell. I'm such a lousy player anyway. Say, I don't mean to be nosy, but does she come visit you much?'

'Actually she hasn't been here at all. But that was always the understanding we had, before I came in here.'

'Yeah?'

She seemed puzzled so I said: 'It might sound odd, I know, but that's the way we wanted to do it.'

'Right.' Then after a while she said: 'So does that mean no one comes to visit you here?'

'I get visitors. Matter of fact, someone called this morning. Musician I used to work with.'

'Oh yeah? That's good. You know, sweetie, I've never been sure how these knights move. If you see me do something wrong, you just say, okay? It's not me trying to pull a fast one.'

'Sure.' Then I said: 'The guy who came to see me today, he told me some news. It was kind of strange. A coincidence.'

'Yeah?'

'There's this saxophone player we both knew a few years back, in San Diego, guy called Jake Marvell. Maybe you've heard of him. He's big-league now. But back then, when we knew him, he was nothing. In fact, he was a phoney. What you'd call a bluffer. Never knew his way around the keys properly. And I've heard him recently, plenty of times, and he hasn't gotten any better. But he's had a few breaks and now he's considered hot. I swear to you he's not one bit better than he used to be, not one bit. And you know what this news was? This same guy, Jake Marvell, he's getting a big music award tomorrow, right here in this hotel. Jazz Musician of the Year. It's just crazy, you know? So many talented sax players out there, and they decide to give it to Jake.'

I made myself stop, and looking up from the chess board, did a little laugh. 'What can you do?' I said, more gently.

Lindy was sitting up, her attention fully on me. 'That's too bad. And this guy, he's no good, you say?'

'I'm sorry, I was kind of out of line there. They want to give Jake an award, why shouldn't they?'

'But if he's no good . . .'

'He's as good as the next guy. I was just talking. I'm sorry, you have to ignore me.'

'Hey, that reminds me,' Lindy said. 'Did you remember to bring your music?'

I indicated the CD beside me on the sofa. 'I don't know if it would interest you. You don't have to listen . . .'

'Oh, but I do, I absolutely do. Here, let me see it.'

I handed her the CD. 'It's a band I played with in Pasadena. We played standards, old-fashioned swing, a little bossa nova. Nothing special, I just brought it because you asked.'

She was examining the CD case, holding it close to her face, then away from her again. 'So are you in this picture?' She brought it up close again. 'I'm kind of curious what you look like. Or I should say, what you *looked* like.'

'I'm second from the right. In the Hawaiian shirt, holding the ironing board.'

'*This* one?' She stared at the CD, then over at me. Then she said: 'Hey, you're cute.' But she said it quietly, in a voice devoid of conviction. In fact, I noted a definite touch of pity there. Almost immediately, though, she'd recovered. 'Okay, so let's hear it!'

As she moved towards the Bang & Olufsen, I said: 'Track number nine. "The Nearness of You". That's my special track.'

'"The Nearness of You" coming up.'

I'd settled on this track after some thought. The musicians in that band had been top-notch. Individually we'd all had more radical ambitions, but we'd formed the band with the express purpose of playing quality mainstream material, the sort the supper crowd would want. Our version of "The Nearness of You" – which featured my tenor all the way through – wasn't a hundred miles from Tony Gardner territory, but I'd always been genuinely proud of it. Maybe you think you've heard this song done every way possible. Well, listen to ours. Listen, say, to that second chorus. Or to that moment as we come out of the middle eight, when the band go III-5 to VIx-9 while I rise up in intervals you'd never believe possible and then hold that sweet, very tender high B-flat. I think there are colors there, longings and regrets, you won't have come across before.

So you could say I was confident this recording would meet with Lindy's approval. And for the first minute or so, she looked to be enjoying herself. She'd stayed on her feet after loading the CD, and just like the time she'd played me her husband's record, she began swaying dreamily to the slow beat. But then the rhythm faded from her movements, until she was standing there quite still, her back to me, head bent forward like she was concentrating. I didn't at first see this as a bad sign. It was only when she came walking back and sat down with the music still in full flow, I realised something was wrong. Because of the bandages, of course, I couldn't read her expression, but the way she let herself slump into the sofa, like a tense mannequin, didn't look good.

When the track ended, I picked up the remote and turned it all off. For what felt a long time, she stayed the way she was, stiff and awkward. Then she hauled herself up a little and began fingering a chess piece.

'That was very nice,' she said. 'Thank you for letting me hear it.' It sounded formulaic, and she didn't seem to mind that it did.

'Maybe it wasn't quite your kind of thing.'

'No, no.' Her voice had become sulky and quiet. 'It was just fine. Thank you for letting me hear it.' She put the chess piece down on a square, then said: 'Your move.'

I looked at the board, trying to remember where we were. After a while, I asked gently: 'Maybe that particular song, it has special associations for you?'

She looked up and I sensed anger behind her bandages. But she said in the same quiet voice: 'That song? It has no associations. None at all.' Suddenly she laughed – a short, unkind laugh. 'Oh, you mean associations with *him*, with Tony? No, no. It was never one of his numbers. You play it very nicely. Really professional.'

'Really *professional*? What's that supposed to mean?'

'I mean . . . that it's really professional. I mean it as a compliment.'

'Professional?' I got to my feet, crossed the room and got the disc out of the machine.

'What are you so mad about?' Her voice was still distant and cold. 'I say something wrong? I'm sorry. I was trying to be nice.'

I came back to the table, put the disc back in its case, but didn't sit down.

'So we going to finish the game?' she asked.

'If you don't mind, I've got a few things I have to do. Phone calls. Paperwork.'

'What are you so mad about? I don't understand.'

'I'm not mad at all. Time's getting on, that's all.'

She at least got to her feet to walk me to the door, where we parted with a cold handshake.

*

I've said already how my sleep rhythm had been screwed up after the surgery. That evening I became suddenly tired, went to bed early, slept soundly for a few hours, then woke in the dead of night unable to go back to sleep. After a while I got up and turned on the TV. I found a movie I'd seen as a kid, so pulled up a chair and watched what remained of it with the volume down low. When that was over I watched two preachers shouting at each other in front of a baying audience. All in all, I was contented. I felt cosy and a million miles from the outside world. So my heart just about jumped out of my chest when the phone rang.

'Steve? That you?' It was Lindy. Her voice sounded odd and I wondered if she'd been drinking.

'Yeah, it's me.'

'I know it's late. But just now, when I was passing, I saw your light on under your door. I supposed you were having trouble sleeping, just like me.'

'I guess so. It's difficult keeping regular hours.'

'Yeah. It sure is.'

'Is everything okay?' I asked.

'Sure. Everything's good. *Very* good.'

I realised now she wasn't drunk, but I couldn't put my finger on what was up with her. She probably wasn't high on anything either – just peculiarly awake and maybe excited about something she had to tell me.

'You sure everything's okay?' I asked again.

'Yeah, really, but . . . Look, sweetie, I have something here, something I want to give to you.'

'Oh? And what might that be?'

'I don't want to say. I want it to be a surprise.'

'Sounds interesting. I'll come and get it, maybe after breakfast?'

'I was kinda hoping you'd come and get it now. I mean, it's here, and you're awake and I'm awake. I know it's late, but . . . Listen, Steve, about earlier, about what happened. I feel I owe you an explanation.'

'Forget it. I didn't mind . . .'

'You were mad at me because you thought I didn't like your music. Well, that wasn't true. That was the reverse of the truth, the exact reverse. What you played me, that version of "Nearness of You"? I haven't been able to get it out of my head. No, I don't mean head, I mean heart. I haven't been able to get it out of my *heart*.'

I didn't know what to say, and before I could think of anything she was talking again.

'Will you come over? Right now? Then I'll explain it all properly. And most important . . . No, no, I'm not saying. It's gonna be a surprise. Come on over and you'll see. And bring your CD again. Will you do that?'

She took the CD from me as soon as she opened the door, like I was the delivery boy, but then grasped me by the wrist and led me in. Lindy was in the same glamorous dressing gown as before, but she looked a little less immaculate now: one side of the gown was hanging lower than the other, and a woolly dangle of fluff was caught on the back of her bandages near the neckline.

'I take it you've been on one of your nocturnal walks,' I said.

'I'm so glad you're up. I don't know if I could have waited till morning. Now listen, like I told you, I have a surprise. I hope you're gonna like it, I think you will. But first I want you to make yourself comfortable. We're gonna listen to your song again. Let me see, which track was it?'

I sat down on my usual sofa and watched her fussing with the hi-fi. The lighting in the room was soft, and the air felt pleasantly cool. Then "The Nearness of You" came on at high volume.

'Don't you think this might disturb people?' I said.

'To hell with them. We pay enough for this place, it's not our problem. Now shhh! Listen, listen!'

She began to sway to the music like before, only this time she didn't stop after a verse. In fact, she seemed to get more lost in the music the longer it went on, holding out her arms like she had an imaginary dance partner. When it finished, she turned it off and remained very still, standing at the end of the room with her back to me. She stayed like that for what felt like a long time, then finally came towards me.

'I don't know what to say,' she said. 'It's sublime. You're a wonderful, wonderful musician. You're a genius.'

'Well, thank you.'

'I knew it the first time. That's the truth. That's why I reacted the way I did. Pretending not to like it, pretending to be snotty?' She sat down facing me and sighed. 'Tony used to pull me up about it. I've always done it, it's something I don't ever seem to get over. I run into a person who's, you know, who's really talented, someone who's just

been blessed that way by God, and I can't help it, my first
instinct is to do what I did with you. It's just, I don't know,
I guess it's jealousy. It's like you see these women sometimes, they're kind of plain? A beautiful woman comes
into the same room, they hate it, they want to claw her eyes
out. That's the way I am when I meet someone like you.
Especially if it's unexpected, the way it was today and I'm
not ready. I mean, there you were, one minute I'm thinking
you're just one of the public, then suddenly you're . . . well,
something else. You know what I'm saying? Anyway, I'm
trying to tell you why I behaved so badly earlier on. You
had every right to be mad at me.'

The late-night silence hung between us for a while.
'Well, I appreciate it,' I said eventually. 'I appreciate you
telling me this.'

She stood up suddenly. 'Now, the surprise! Just wait
there, don't move.'

She went through into the adjoining room and I could
hear her opening and shutting drawers. When she came
back, she was holding something in front of her with both
hands, but I couldn't see what the something was, because
she'd thrown a silk handkerchief over it. She halted in the
middle of the room.

'Steve, I want you to come and receive this. This is going
to be a presentation.'

I was puzzled, but got to my feet. As I went to her, she
pulled off the handkerchief and held towards me a shiny
brass ornament.

'You thoroughly deserve this. So it's yours. Jazz
Musician of the Year. Maybe of all time. Congratulations.'

She placed it in my hands and kissed me lightly on the cheek through the crêpe.

'Well, thanks. This *is* a surprise. Hey, this looks pretty. What is it? An alligator?'

'An alligator? Come on! It's a pair of cute little cherubs kissing each other.'

'Oh yeah, I can see it now. Well, thanks, Lindy. I don't know what to say. It's really beautiful.'

'An alligator!'

'I'm sorry. It's just the way this guy has his leg stretched all the way out. But I see now. It's really beautiful.'

'Well, it's yours. You deserve it.'

'I'm touched, Lindy. I really am. And what does this say down here? I don't have my glasses.'

'It says "Jazz Musician of the Year". What else would it say?'

'That's what it says?'

'Sure, that's what it says.'

I went back to the sofa, holding the statuette, sat down and thought a little. 'Say, Lindy,' I said eventually. 'This item you've just given me. It's not possible, is it, you came across it on one of your midnight walks?'

'Sure. Sure it's possible.'

'I see. And it's not possible, is it, this is the real award? I mean the actual gong they were going to hand to Jake?'

Lindy didn't reply for a few seconds, but kept standing there very still. Then she said:

'Of course it's the real thing. What would be the point, giving you any old junk? There was an injustice about to be committed, but now justice has prevailed. That's all that matters. Hey, sweetie, come on. You know you're the one who deserves this award.'

'I appreciate your viewpoint. It's just that . . . well, this is kind of like stealing.'

'Stealing? Didn't you say yourself this guy's no good? A fake? And you're a genius. Who's trying to steal from who here?'

'Lindy, where exactly did you come across this thing?'

She shrugged. 'Just some place. One of the places I go. An office, you'd call it maybe.'

'Tonight? You picked it up tonight?'

'Of course I picked it up tonight. I didn't know about your award last night.'

'Sure, sure. So that was an hour ago, would you say?'

'An hour. Maybe two hours. Who knows? I was out there some time. I went to my presidential suite for a while.'

'Jesus.'

'Look, who cares? What are you so worried about? They lose this one, they can just go get another one. They've probably got a closet full somewhere. I presented you with something you deserve. You're not going to turn it down, are you, Steve?'

'I'm not turning it down, Lindy. The sentiment, the honor, all of that, I accept it all, I'm really happy about it. But this, the actual trophy. We're going to have to take it back. We'll have to put it back exactly where you found it.'

'Screw them! Who cares?'

'Lindy, you haven't thought this through. What will you do when this gets out? Can you imagine what the press will do with this? The gossip, the scandal? What will your public say? Now come on. We're going out there right now before people start waking up. You're going to show me exactly where you found this thing.'

She suddenly looked like a kid who'd been scolded. Then she sighed and said: 'I guess you're right, sweetie.'

Once we'd agreed to take it back, Lindy became quite possessive about the award, holding it close to her bosom all the time we hurried through the passageways of the vast, sleeping hotel. She led the way down hidden stairways, along back corridors, past sauna rooms and vending machines. We didn't see or hear a soul. Then Lindy whispered: 'It was this way,' and we pushed through heavy doors into a dark space.

Once I was sure we were alone, I switched on the flashlight I'd brought from Lindy's room and shone it around. We were in the ballroom, though if you were looking to dance just then, you'd have had trouble with all the dining tables, each one with its white linen cover and matching chairs. The ceiling had a fancy central chandelier. At the far end there was a raised stage, probably large enough to put on a fair-sized show, though right now the curtains were drawn across it. Someone had left a step-ladder in the middle of the room and an upright vacuum cleaner against the wall.

'It's going to be some party,' she said. 'Four hundred, five hundred people?'

I wandered further into the room and threw the torch beam around some more. 'Maybe this is where it's going to happen. Where they're going to give Jake his award.'

'Of course it is. Where I found this' – she held up the statuette – 'there were other ones too. Best Newcomer. R&B Album of the Year. That kind of stuff. It's going to be a big event.'

Now my eyes had adjusted, I could see the place better, even though the flashlight wasn't so powerful. And for a moment, as I stood there looking up at the stage, I could imagine the way the place would look later on. I imagined all the people in their fancy clothes, the record-company men, the big-time promoters, the random showbiz celebrities, laughing and praising each other; the fawningly sincere applause every time the MC mentioned the name of a sponsor; more applause, this time with whoops and cheers, when the award winners went up. I imagined Jake Marvell up on that stage, holding his trophy, the same smug smile he'd always have in San Diego when he'd finished a solo and the audience had clapped.

'Maybe we've got this wrong,' I said. 'Maybe there's no need to return this. Maybe we should throw it in the garbage. And all the other awards you found with it.'

'Yeah?' Lindy sounded puzzled. 'Is that what you want to do, sweetie?'

I let out a sigh. 'No, I guess not. But it would be . . . satisfying, wouldn't it? All those awards in the garbage. I bet every one of those winners is a fake. I bet there isn't enough talent between the lot of them to fill a hot-dog bun.'

I waited for Lindy to say something to this, but nothing came. Then when she did speak, there was some new note, something tighter, in her voice.

'How do you know some of these guys aren't okay? How do you know some of them don't deserve their award?'

'How do I know?' I felt a sudden tide of irritation. 'How do I know? Well, think about it. A panel that considers Jake Marvell the year's outstanding jazz musician. What other kind of people are they going to honor?'

'But what do you know about these guys? Even this Jake fella. How do you know he didn't work really hard to get where he has?'

'What is this? You're Jake's greatest fan now?'

'I'm just expressing my opinion.'

'Your opinion? So this is your opinion? I guess I should-n't be so surprised. For a moment there, I was forgetting who you were.'

'What the hell's that supposed to mean? How dare you speak to me that way?!'

It occurred to me I was losing my grip. I said quickly: 'Okay, I'm out of line. I'm sorry. Now let's go find this office.'

Lindy had gone silent, and when I turned to face her, I couldn't see well enough in the light to guess what she was thinking.

'Lindy, where's this office? We need to find it.'

Eventually, she indicated with the statuette towards the back of the hall, then led the way past the tables, still not speaking. When we were there, I put my ear against the door for a few seconds, and hearing nothing, opened it carefully.

We were in a long narrow space that seemed to run par-allel with the ballroom. A dim light had been left on somewhere, so we could just about make things out without the flashlight. It was obviously not the office we were after, but some kind of catering-cum-kitchen area. Long extended work counters ran along both walls, leaving a gangway down the middle wide enough for staff to put final touches to the food.

But Lindy seemed to recognise the place and went striding purposefully down the gangway. About halfway along, she stopped suddenly to examine one of the baking trays left on the counter.

'Hey, cookies!' She seemed completely to have regained her equanimity. 'Too bad it's all under cellophane. I'm famished. Look! Let's see what's under this one.'

She went on a few more steps, to a big dome-shaped lid, and raised it. 'Look at this, sweetie. This looks *really* good.'

She was leaning over a plump roast turkey. Instead of replacing the lid, she laid it down carefully next to the bird.

'Do you think they'd mind if I pulled off a leg?'

'I think they'd mind a lot, Lindy. But what the hell.'

'It's a big baby. You want to share a leg with me?'

'Sure, why not?'

'Okay. Here goes.'

She reached towards the turkey. Then suddenly she straightened and turned to face me.

'So what was that supposed to mean back there?'

'What was what supposed to mean?'

'What you were saying. When you said you weren't surprised. About my opinion. What was that about?'

'Look, I'm sorry. I wasn't trying to be offensive. Just thinking aloud, that's all.'

[165]

'Thinking aloud? Well, how about thinking aloud some more? So I suggest some of these guys may have deserved their awards, why is that a ridiculous statement?'

'Look, all I'm saying is that the wrong people end up with the awards. That's all. But you seem to know better. You think that's not what happens . . .'

'Some of those guys, maybe they worked damn hard to get where they have. And maybe they deserve a little recognition. The trouble with people like you, just because God's given you this special gift, you think that entitles you to everything. That you're better than the rest of us, that you deserve to go to the front of the line every time. You don't see there's a whole lot of other people weren't as lucky as you who work really hard for their place in the world . . .'

'So you don't think I work hard? You think I sit on my ass all day? I sweat and heave and break my balls to come up with something worthwhile, something beautiful, then who is it gets the recognition? Jake Marvell! People like you!'

'How fucking dare you! What do I have to do with this? Am I getting an award today? Has anyone *ever* given me a goddamn award? Have I ever had anything, even in school, one lousy certificate for singing or dancing or any damn thing else? No! Not a fucking thing! I had to watch all of you, all you creeps, going up there, getting the prizes, and all the parents clapping . . .'

'No prizes? No prizes? Look at you! Who gets to be famous? Who gets the fancy houses . . .'

At that moment someone flicked a switch and we were

blinking at each other under harsh bright lights. Two men had come in the same way we had, and were now moving towards us. The gangway was just wide enough to let them walk side by side. One was a huge black guy in a hotel security guard's uniform, and what I first thought was a gun in his hand was a two-way radio. Beside him was a small white man in a light-blue suit with slick black hair. Neither of them looked particularly deferential. They stopped a yard or two away, then the small guy took an ID out of his jacket.

'LAPD,' he said. 'Name's Morgan.'

'Good evening,' I said.

For a moment the cop and the security guard went on looking at us in silence. Then the cop asked:

'Guests of the hotel?'

'Yes, we are,' I said. 'We're guests.'

I felt the soft material of Lindy's night-gown brush against my back. Then she'd taken my arm and we were standing side by side.

'Good evening, officer,' she said in a sleepy, honeydew voice quite unlike her usual one.

'Good evening, ma'am,' the cop said. 'And are you folks up at this time for any special reason?'

We both started to answer at once, then laughed. But neither of the men laughed or smiled.

'We were having trouble sleeping,' Lindy said. 'So we were just walking.'

'Just walking.' The cop looked around in the stark white light. 'Maybe looking for something to eat.'

'That's right, officer!' Lindy's voice was still way over the top. 'We got a little hungry, the way I'm sure you do too sometimes in the night.'

'I guess room service isn't up to much,' the cop said.

'No, it's not so good,' I said.

'Just the usual stuff,' the cop said. 'Steaks, pizzas, hamburgers, triple-decker clubs. I know because I just ordered from all-night room service myself. But I guess you folks don't like that kind of food.'

'Well, you know how it is, officer,' Lindy said. 'It's the *fun*. The fun of creeping down and taking a bite, you know, a little bit forbidden, the way you did when you were a kid?'

Neither men showed any sign of melting. But the cop said:

'Sorry to trouble you folks. But you understand this area isn't open to guests. And one or two items have gone missing just lately.'

'Really?'

'Yeah. You folks see anything odd or suspicious tonight?'

Lindy and I looked at each other, then she shook her head at me dramatically.

'No,' I said. 'We haven't seen anything odd.'

'Nothing at all?'

The security guard had been coming closer, and now he came past us, squeezing his bulk along the counter. I realised the plan was for him to check us over more closely, to see if maybe we were concealing anything on our persons, while his partner kept us talking.

'No, nothing,' I said. 'What kind of thing did you have in mind?'

'Suspicious people. Unusual activity.'

'Do you mean, officer,' Lindy said with shocked horror, 'that rooms have been broken into?'

'Not exactly, ma'am. But certain items of value have gone missing.'

I could sense the security guard shift behind us.

'So that's why you're here with us,' Lindy said. 'To protect us and our belongings.'

'That's right, ma'am.' The cop's gaze moved fractionally, and I got the impression he'd exchanged a look with the man behind us. 'So if you see anything odd, please call security right away.'

The interview seemed to be over and the cop moved aside to let us out. Relieved, I made a move to go, but Lindy said:

'I suppose it was kind of naughty of us, coming down here to eat. We thought about helping ourselves to some of that gateau over there, but then we thought it might be for a special occasion and it would be such a shame to spoil it.'

'This hotel has good room service,' the cop said. 'Twenty-four hours.'

I tugged at Lindy, but she seemed now to be seized by the oft-cited mania of criminals to flirt with being caught.

'And you just ordered something up yourself, officer?'

'Sure.'

'And was it good?'

'It was pretty good. I recommend you folks do the same.'

'Let's leave these gentlemen to get on with their investigations,' I said, tugging at her arm. But still she didn't budge.

'Officer, may I ask you something?' she asked. 'Do you mind?'

'Try me.'

'You were talking just now about seeing something odd. You see anything odd yourself? I mean, about us?'

'I don't know what you mean, ma'am.'

'Like we both of us have our faces entirely wrapped in bandages? Did you notice that?'

The cop looked at us carefully, as though to verify this last statement. Then he said: 'As a matter of fact, I did notice, ma'am, yes. But I didn't wish to make personal remarks.'

'Oh, I see,' Lindy said. Then turning to me: 'Wasn't that considerate of him?'

'Come on,' I said, pulling her along now quite forcefully. I could feel both men staring at our backs all the way to the exit.

We crossed the ballroom with an outward show of calm. But once we were past the big swing doors, we gave in to panic and broke into a near-run. Our arms stayed linked, so we did a lot of stumbling and colliding as Lindy led me through the building. Then she pulled me into a service elevator, and only when the doors closed and we were climbing did she let go, lean back against the metal wall and start up a weird noise, which I realised was how hysterical laughter sounds coming through bandages.

When we stepped out of the elevator, she put her arm through mine again. 'Okay, we're safe,' she said. 'Now I want to take you somewhere. This is really something. See this?' She was holding up a key card. 'Let's see what this can do for us.'

She used the card to get us through a door marked 'Private', then a door marked 'Danger. Keep Out.' Then we were standing in a space smelling of paint and plaster. There were cables dangling from the walls and ceiling, and the cold floor was splashed and mottled. We could see fine because one side of the room was entirely glass – unadorned by curtains or blinds – and all the outdoor lighting was filling the place with yellowish patches. We were up even higher than on our floor: there was in front of us a helicopter-style view over the freeway and the surrounding territory.

'It's going to be a new presidential suite,' Lindy said. 'I love coming here. No light switches yet, no carpet. But it's slowly coming together. When I first found it, it was much rougher. Now you can see how it'll look. There's even this couch now.'

In the centre of the room was a bulky shape with a sheet draped completely over it. Lindy went to it like it was an old friend and flopped down tiredly.

'It's my fantasy,' she said, 'but I kind of believe in it. They're building this room just for me. That's why I get to be in here. All of this. It's because they're helping me. Helping me build my future. This place used to be a real mess. But look at it now. It's taking shape. It's gonna be grand.' She patted the space next to her. 'Come on, sweetie, have a rest. I'm feeling drained. You must be too.'

The couch – or whatever it was under the sheet – was surprisingly comfortable, and as soon as I'd sunk into it, I felt waves of tiredness coming over me.

'Boy, am I sleepy,' Lindy said, and her weight fell onto

my shoulder. 'Isn't this a great place? I found the key in the slot, first time I came here.'

We were quiet for a while, and I felt myself falling asleep. But then I remembered something.

'Hey, Lindy.'

'Mmm?'

'Lindy. What happened to that award?'

'The award? Oh yeah. The award. I hid it. What else could I do? You know, sweetie, you really deserved that award. I hope it means something to you, my presenting it to you tonight, the way I did. It wasn't just a whim. I thought about it. I thought about it really carefully. I don't know if it means much to you. I don't know if you'll even remember it ten years, twenty years down the line.'

'I will for sure. And it does mean a lot to me. But Lindy, you say you hid it, but where? Where did you hide it?'

'Mmm?' She was falling asleep again. 'I hid it the only place I could. I put it in that turkey.'

'You put it in the turkey.'

'I did exactly the same thing once when I was nine years old. I hid my sister's glowball inside a turkey. That's what gave me the idea. Quick thinking, right?'

'Yeah, it sure was.' I felt so tired, but I forced myself to focus. 'But Lindy, how well did you hide it? I mean, would those cops have found it by now?'

'I don't see how. There wasn't anything sticking out, if that's what you mean. Why would they think to look up there? I was pushing it behind my back, like this. And kept pushing. I didn't turn around to look at it, because then those boys would have wondered what I was doing. It wasn't just a whim, you know. Deciding to give you that award. I thought about it, real hard. I sure hope it means something to you. God, I need to sleep.'

She slumped against me and the next moment she was making snoring noises. Concerned about her surgery, I adjusted her head carefully so her cheek wasn't pressing on my shoulder. Then I too began to drift off.

I woke with a jerk and saw signs of dawn in the big window in front of us. Lindy was still fast asleep, so I carefully extricated myself from her, stood up and stretched my arms. I went to the window and looked at the pale sky and the freeway far below. Something had been on my mind as I was falling asleep and I tried to remember what it was, but my brain was foggy and exhausted. Then I remembered, and I went to the couch and shook Lindy awake.

'What is it? What is it? Whaddaya want?' she said without opening her eyes.

'Lindy,' I said. 'The award. We've forgotten about the award.'

'I told you already. It's in that turkey.'

'Okay, so listen. Those cops may not have thought to look inside the turkey. But sooner or later, someone's going to find it. Maybe someone's carving it right now.'

'So what? So they find the thing in there. So what?'

'They find the thing in there, they report the big find. Then that cop remembers us. He remembers we were there, standing next to that turkey.'

Lindy seemed to get more awake. 'Yeah,' she said. 'I see what you're saying.'

'While that trophy stays in the turkey, they can link us to the crime.'

'Crime? Hey, what do you mean crime?'

'Doesn't matter what you call it. We need to go back there and get that thing out of the turkey. It doesn't matter where we leave it after that. But we can't leave it where it is now.'

'Sweetie, are you sure we have to do this? I'm so tired now.'

'We have to do it, Lindy. We leave it the way it is, you'll get in trouble. And remember that means a big story for the press.'

Lindy thought about this, then she straightened up her posture a few notches and looked up at me. 'Okay,' she said. 'Let's go back there.'

This time round there were cleaning noises and voices down corridors, but we still made it back to the ballroom without encountering anyone. There was also more light to see by, and Lindy pointed out the notice beside the double doors. It said in plastic mix-and-spell letters: J. A. POOL CLEANSERS INC BREAKFAST.

'No wonder we couldn't find that office with all the awards,' she said. 'This is the wrong ballroom.'

'It makes no difference. What we want is in there now.'

We crossed the ballroom, then cautiously entered the catering room. Like before, a dim light had been left on, and now there was also some natural light from the ventilation windows. There was nobody in sight, but when I glanced along the work counters, I saw we were in trouble.

'Looks like someone's been here,' I said.

'Yeah.' Lindy took a few steps down the gangway, glancing about her. 'Yeah. Looks that way.'

All the canisters, trays, cake-boxes, silver-domed platters we'd seen earlier had vanished. In their place were neat piles of plates and napkins positioned at regular intervals.

'Okay, so they've moved all the food,' I said. 'Question is, where to?'

Lindy wandered further down the gangway, then turned to me. 'Remember, Steve, the last time we were here, before those men came in? We were having quite a discussion.'

'Yeah, I remember. But why go over that again? I know I was out of line.'

'Yeah right, let's forget it. So where's that turkey gone?' She glanced around some more. 'You know what, Steve? When I was a kid, I so wanted to be a dancer and a singer. And I tried and tried, God knows I tried, but people just laughed, and I thought, this world is so unfair. But then I grew up a little and I realised the world wasn't so unfair after all. That even if you were like me, one of the unblessed, there was still a chance for you, you could still find a place in the sun, you didn't have to settle for being just *public*. It wasn't going to be easy. You'd have to work at it, not mind what people said. But there was definitely still a chance.'

'Well, it looks like you did okay.'

'It's funny the way this world works. You know, I think it was very insightful. On the part of your wife, I mean. Telling you to get this surgery.'

'Let's leave her out of it. Hey, Lindy, do you know where that leads? Over there?'

At the far end of the room, where the counters came to an end, there were three steps leading up to a green door.

'Why don't we try it?' Lindy said.

We opened the door as cautiously as the last one, then for a while I became utterly disoriented. Everything was very dark and each time I tried to turn I found I was beating back curtain material or else tarpaulin. Lindy, who'd taken the flashlight, seemed to be doing better somewhere in front of me. Then I stumbled out into a dark space, where she was waiting for me, shining the torch at my feet.

'I've noticed,' she said, in a whisper. 'You don't like talking about her. Your wife, I mean.'

'It's not that exactly,' I whispered back. 'Where are we?'

'And she never comes to visit.'

'That's because we're not exactly together just now. Since you must know.'

'Oh, I'm sorry. I didn't mean to be nosy.'

'You didn't mean to be nosy?!'

'Hey, sweetie, look! This is it! We've found it!'

She was pointing the beam at a table a short distance away. It had a white tablecloth on it, and two silver domes side by side.

I went up to the first dome and carefully raised it. Sure enough, there was a fat roast turkey sitting there. I searched out its cavity and inserted a finger.

'Nothing here,' I said.

'You have to get right in there. I pushed it right up. These birds are bigger than you think.'

'I'm telling you there's nothing in there. Hold the flashlight over here. We'll try this other one.' I carefully took the lid off the second turkey.

'You know, Steve, I think it's a mistake. You shouldn't be embarrassed to talk about it.'

'Talk about what?'

'About you and your wife being separated.'

'Did I say we were separated? Did I say that?'

'I thought . . .'

'I said we weren't exactly together. That's not the same thing.'

'It sounds the same thing . . .'

'Well, it isn't. It's just a temporary thing, something we're trying out. Hey, I've got something. There's something in here. This is it.'

'Then why don't you pull it out, sweetie?'

'What do you think I'm trying to do?! Jesus! Did you have to push it in so far?'

'Sssh! There's someone out there!'

At first it was hard to say how many of them there were. Then the voice came closer and I realised it was just the one guy, talking continuously into a cellphone. I also realised exactly where we were. I'd been thinking we'd wandered into some vague backstage area, but in fact we were up on the stage itself, and the curtain facing me was the only thing now dividing us from the ballroom. The man on the cellphone, then, was walking across the floor of the ballroom towards the stage.

I whispered to Lindy to turn off the flashlight and it went dark. She said into my ear: 'Let's get out of here,' and I could hear her creeping away. I tried again to pull the statuette out of the turkey, but now I was afraid of making noise, and besides, my fingers just couldn't get any purchase.

The voice kept coming closer until it felt like the guy was right there in front of me.

'. . . It's not my problem, Larry. We need the logos to be on these menu cards. I don't care how you do it. Okay, then you do it yourself. That's right, you do it yourself, bring them over yourself, I don't care how you do it. Just get them here this morning, seven-thirty latest. We need those things here. The tables look fine. There are plenty of tables, trust me. Okay. I'll check that out. Okay, okay. Yeah. I'm gonna check that out right now.'

For the last part of this, his voice had been moving over to one side of the room. He must now have flicked a switch on some wall panel, because a strong beam came on directly above me, and also a whirring noise like the air-conditioning had come on. Only I realised the noise wasn't the air-conditioning, but the curtains opening in front of me.

Twice in my career I've had it happen when I've been on stage, I've had a solo to play, and suddenly it hits me I don't know how to start, which key I'm in, how the chords change. On both occasions this happened, I just froze up, like I was in a still from a movie, until one of the other boys stepped in to the rescue. It's only happened twice in over twenty years of playing professionally. Anyway, this is how I reacted to the spotlight coming on above me and the curtains starting to move. I just froze. And I felt oddly detached. I felt a kind of mild curiosity concerning what I'd see once the curtain was gone.

[178]

What I saw was the ballroom, and from the vantage
point of the stage, I could appreciate better the way the
tables were laid out in two parallel lines all the way to the
back. The spot above me was putting the room in shade a
little, but I could make out the chandelier and the fancy
ceiling.

The cellphone man was an overweight bald guy in a pale
suit and open-neck shirt. He must have walked away from
the wall as soon as he'd flicked the switch, because now he
was more or less level with me. He had his phone pressed
to his ear, and from his expression you'd guess he was listening with extra attention to what was being said at the
other end. But I supposed he wasn't, because his eyes were
fixed on me. He kept looking at me and I kept looking at
him, and the situation might have gone on indefinitely if
he hadn't said into the phone, maybe in response to a query
about why he'd gone silent:

'It's all right. It's all right. It's a man.' There was a pause,
then he said: 'I thought for a moment it was something
else. But it's a man. With a bandaged head, wearing a
night-gown. That's all it is, I see it now. It's just that he's
got a chicken or something on the end of his arm.'

Straightening up, I instinctively started to stretch out
my arms in a shrugging motion. My right hand still being
inside the turkey beyond the wrist, the sheer weight
brought the whole arrangement back down with a crash.
But at least I'd no more worries about concealment, so I
went right at it, no holds barred, in an effort to extricate
both my hand and the statuette. Meanwhile the man went
on talking into his phone.

[179]

'No, it's exactly what I say. And now he's taking his chicken off. Oh, and he's producing something out of it. Hey, fella, what *is* that? An alligator?'

These last words he'd addressed to me with admirable nonchalance. But now I had the statuette in my hands and the turkey fell to the floor with a thud. As I hurried towards the darkness behind me, I heard the man say to his friend:

'How the hell do I know? Some kind of magic show maybe.'

I don't remember how we got back to our floor. I was lost again in a mess of curtains coming off the stage, then she was there pulling me by the hand. Next thing, we were hurrying through the hotel, no longer caring how much noise we made or who saw us. Somewhere along the way I left the statuette on a room-service tray outside a bedroom, beside the remains of someone's supper.

Back in her room, we flopped down into a sofa and laughed. We laughed till we were collapsing into each other, then she got up, went to the window and raised the blinds. It was now light outside, though the morning was overcast. She went to her cabinet to mix drinks – 'the world's sexiest alcohol-free cocktail' – and brought me over a glass. I thought she'd sit down beside me, but she drifted back towards the window, sipping from her own glass.

'You looking forward to it, Steve?' she asked after a while. 'To the bandages coming off?'

'Yeah. I suppose so.'

'Even last week, I didn't think about it so much. It seemed such a long way off. But now it's not so long.'

'That's right,' I said. 'It's not long for me either.' Then I said quietly: 'Jesus.'

She sipped her drink and looked out of the window. Then I heard her say: 'Hey, sweetie, what's the matter with you?'

'I'm fine. I just need to get some sleep, that's all.'

She kept looking at me for a while. 'I tell you, Steve,' she said eventually. 'It's gonna be fine. Boris is the best. You'll see.'

'Yeah.'

'Hey, what's wrong with you? Listen, this is my third time. Second time with Boris. It's gonna be just fine. You're gonna look great, just great. And your career. From here it's gonna rocket.'

'Maybe.'

'No maybe about it! It'll make such a difference, believe me. You'll be in magazines, you'll be on TV.'

I said nothing to this.

'Hey, come on!' She took a few steps towards me. 'Cheer up there. You're not still mad at me, are you? We were a great team down there, weren't we? And I'll tell you something else. From now on I'm gonna stay part of your team. You're a goddamn genius, and I'm gonna make sure things go well for you.'

'It won't work, Lindy.' I shook my head. 'It won't work.'

'Like hell it won't work. I'll talk to people. People who can do you a lot of good.'

I kept shaking my head. 'I appreciate it. But it's no use. It won't work. It was never going to work. I should never have listened to Bradley.'

'Hey, come on. I may not be married to Tony anymore, but I still have a lot of good friends in this town.'

'Sure, Lindy, I know that. But it's no use. You see, Bradley, that's my manager, he talked me into this whole thing. I was an idiot to listen to him, but I couldn't help it. I was at my wit's end, and then he came out with this theory. He said my wife, Helen, she had this scheme. She hadn't really left me. No, it was all part of this scheme she had. She was doing it all for me, to make it possible for me to get this surgery. And when the bandages came off, and I had a new face, she'd come back and it'd be all right again. That's what Bradley said. Even when he was saying it, I knew it was bullshit, but what could I do? It was some kind of hope at least. Bradley used it, he used it, he's like that, you know? He's lowlife. All he thinks about is business. And about the big league. What does he care if she comes back or not?'

I stopped and she didn't say anything for a long time. Then she said:

'Look, sweetie, listen. I hope your wife comes back. I really do. But if she doesn't, well, you've just got to start getting some perspective. She might be a great person, but life's so much bigger than just loving someone. You got to get out there, Steve. Someone like you, you don't belong with the public. Look at me. When these bandages come off, am I really going to look the way I did twenty years ago? I don't know. And it's a long time since I was last between husbands. But I'm going to go out there anyway and give it a go.' She came over to me and shoved me on the shoulder. 'Hey. You're just tired. You'll feel a lot better after some sleep. Listen. Boris is the best. He'll have fixed it, for the both of us. You just see.'

I put my glass down on the table and stood up. 'I guess you're right. Like you say, Boris is the best. And we *were* a good team down there.'

'We were a *great* team down there.'

I reached forward, put my hands on her shoulders, then kissed each of her bandaged cheeks. 'You have yourself a good sleep,' I said. 'I'll come over soon and we'll play more chess.'

But after that morning, we didn't see much more of each other. When I thought about it later, it occurred to me there'd been some things said during the course of that night, things I should maybe have apologised about, or at least tried to explain. At the time, though, once we'd made it back to her room, and we'd been laughing together on the sofa, it hadn't seemed necessary, or even right, to bring all of that up again. When we parted that morning, I thought the two of us were well beyond that stage. Even so, I'd seen how Lindy could switch. Maybe later on, she thought back and got mad at me all over again. Who knows? Anyway, though I'd expected a call from her later that day, it never came, and neither did one come the day after. Instead, I heard Tony Gardner records through the wall, playing at top volume, one after the next.

When I did eventually go round there, maybe four days later, she was welcoming, but distant. Like that first time, she talked a lot about her famous friends – though none of it about getting them to help with my career. Still, I didn't mind that. We gave chess a try, but her phone kept ringing and she'd go into the bedroom to talk.

Then two evenings ago she knocked on my door and said she was about to check out. Boris was pleased with her and had agreed to take the bandages off in her own house. We said our goodbyes in a friendly way, but it was like our real goodbyes had been said already, that morning right after our escapade, when I'd reached forward and kissed her on both cheeks.

So that's the story of my time as Lindy Gardner's neighbor. I wish her well. As for me, it's six more days till my own unveiling, and a lot longer still before I'm allowed to blow a horn. But I'm used to this life now, and I pass the hours quite contentedly. Yesterday I got a call from Helen asking how I was doing, and when I told her I'd gotten to know Lindy Gardner, she was mightily impressed.

'Hasn't she married again?' she asked. And when I put her straight on that, she said: 'Oh, right. I must have been thinking about that other one. You know. What's-her-name.'

We talked a lot of unimportant stuff – what she'd watched on TV, how her friend had stopped by with her baby. Then she said Prendergast was asking for me, and when she said that, there was a noticeable tightening in her voice. And I almost said: 'Hello? Do I detect a note of irritation associated with lover boy's name?' But I didn't. I just said to say hi to him, and she didn't bring him up again. I'd probably imagined it anyway. For all I know, she was just angling for me to say how grateful I was to him.

When she was about to go, I said: 'I love you,' in that

fast, routine way you say it at the end of a call with a spouse. There was a silence of a few seconds, then she said it back, in the same routine way. Then she was gone. God knows what that meant. There's nothing to do now, I guess, but wait for these bandages to come off. And then what? Maybe Lindy's right. Maybe, like she says, I need some perspective, and life really is much bigger than loving a person. Maybe this really is a turning point for me, and the big league's waiting. Maybe she's right.

CELLISTS

IT WAS OUR THIRD TIME playing the *Godfather* theme since lunch, so I was looking around at the tourists seated across the piazza to see how many of them might have been there the last time we'd played it. People don't mind hearing a favourite more than once, but you can't have it happen too often or they start suspecting you don't have a decent repertoire. At this time of year, it's usually okay to repeat numbers. The first hint of an autumn wind and the ridiculous price of a coffee ensure a pretty steady turnover of customers. Anyway, that's why I was studying the faces in the piazza and that's how I spotted Tibor.

He was waving his arm and I thought at first he was waving to us, but then I realised he was trying to attract a waiter. He looked older, and he'd put on some weight, but he wasn't hard to recognise. I gave Fabian, on accordion right next to me, a little nudge and nodded towards the young man, though I couldn't take either hand off my saxophone just then to point him out properly. That was when it came home to me, looking around the band, that apart from me and Fabian, there was no one left in our line-up from that summer we'd met Tibor.

Okay, that was all of seven years ago, but it was still a

shock. Playing together every day like this, you come to think of the band as a kind of family, the other members as your brothers. And if every now and then someone moves on, you want to think he'll always stay in touch, sending back postcards from Venice or London or wherever he's got to, maybe a polaroid of the band he's in now – just like he's writing home to his old village. So a moment like that comes as an unwelcome reminder of how quickly things change. How the bosom pals of today become lost strangers tomorrow, scattered across Europe, playing the *Godfather* theme or 'Autumn Leaves' in squares and cafes you'll never visit.

When we finished our number, Fabian gave me a dirty look, annoyed I'd nudged him during his 'special passage' – not a solo exactly, but one of those rare moments when the violin and clarinet have stopped, I'm blowing just quiet notes in the background, and he's holding the tune together on his accordion. When I tried to explain, pointing out Tibor, now stirring his coffee beneath a parasol, Fabian seemed to have trouble remembering him. In the end, he said:

'Ah yes, the boy with the cello. I wonder if he's still with that American woman.'

'Of course not,' I said. 'Don't you remember? That all came to an end at the time.'

Fabian shrugged, his attention now on his sheet music, and then we were starting our next number.

I was disappointed Fabian hadn't shown more interest, but I suppose he'd never been one of those particularly concerned about the young cellist. Fabian, you see, he's only ever played in bars and cafes. Not like Giancarlo, our violin player at that time, or Ernesto, who was our bass player. They'd had formal training, so to them someone like Tibor was always fascinating. Maybe there was a tiny bit of jealousy there – of Tibor's top-drawer musical education, of the fact that his future was still in front of him. But to be fair, I think it was just that they liked to take the Tibors of this world under their wing, look after them a little, maybe prepare them for what lay ahead, so when the disappointments came they wouldn't be quite so hard to take.

That summer seven years ago had been an unusually warm one, and even in this city of ours, there were times you could believe we were down on the Adriatic. We played outdoors for over four months – under the cafe awning, facing out to the piazza and all the tables – and I can tell you that's hot work, even with two or three electric fans whirring around you. But it made for a good season, plenty of tourists passing through, a lot from Germany and Austria, as well as natives fleeing the heat down on the beaches. And that was the summer we first started noticing Russians. Today you don't think twice about Russian tourists, they look like everyone else. But back then, they were still rare enough to make you stop and stare. Their clothes were odd and they moved around like new kids at school. The first time we saw Tibor, we were between sets, refreshing ourselves at the big table the cafe always kept aside for us. He was sitting nearby, continually getting up and re-positioning his cello case to keep it in the shade.

'Look at him,' Giancarlo said. 'A Russian music student

with nothing to live on. So what does he do? Decides to waste his money on coffees in the main square.'

'No doubt a fool,' Ernesto said. 'But a romantic fool. Happy to starve, so long as he can sit in our square all afternoon.'

He was thin, sandy-haired and wore unfashionable spectacles – huge frames that made him look like a panda. He turned up day after day, and I don't remember how exactly it happened, but after a while we began to sit and talk with him in between sets. And sometimes if he came to the cafe during our evening session, we'd call him over afterwards, maybe treat him to some wine and crostini.

We soon discovered Tibor was Hungarian, not Russian; that he was probably older than he looked, because he'd already studied at the Royal Academy of Music in London, then spent two years in Vienna under Oleg Petrovic. After a rocky start with the old maestro, he'd learnt to handle those legendary temper tantrums and had left Vienna full of confidence – and with a series of engagements in prestigious, if small, venues around Europe. But then concerts began to get cancelled due to low demand; he'd been forced to perform music he hated; accommodation had proved expensive or sordid.

So our city's well-organised Arts and Culture Festival – which was what brought him here that summer – had been a much-needed boost, and when an old friend from the Royal Academy had offered him a free apartment for the summer down near the canal, he'd taken it up without hesitation. He was enjoying our city, he told us, but cash was always a problem, and though he'd had the occasional recital, he was now having to think hard about his next move.

It was after a while of listening to these worries that Giancarlo and Ernesto decided we should try and do something for him. And that was how Tibor got to meet Mr Kaufmann, from Amsterdam, a distant relative of Giancarlo's with connections in the hotel world.

I remember that evening very well. It was still early in the summer, and Mr Kaufmann, Giancarlo, Ernesto, all the rest of us, we sat indoors, in the back room of the cafe, listening to Tibor play his cello. The young man must have realised he was auditioning for Mr Kaufmann, so it's interesting now to remember how keen he was to perform that night. He was obviously grateful to us, and you could see he was pleased when Mr Kaufmann promised to do what he could for him on his return to Amsterdam. When people say Tibor changed for the worse that summer, that his head got too big for his own good, that this was all down to the American woman, well, maybe there's something in that.

Tibor had become aware of the woman while sipping his first coffee of the day. At that moment, the piazza was pleasantly cool – the cafe end remains shaded for much of the morning – and the paving stones were still wet from the city workers' hoses. Having gone without breakfast, he'd watched enviously while at the next table she'd ordered a series of fruit-juice concoctions, then – apparently on a whim, for it wasn't yet ten o'clock – a bowl of steamed mussels. He had the vague impression the woman was, for her part, stealing glances back at him, but hadn't thought too much about it.

'She looked very pleasant, beautiful even,' he told us at the time. 'But as you see, she's ten, fifteen years older than me. So why would I think anything was going on?'

He'd forgotten about her and was preparing to get back to his room for a couple of hours' practice before his neighbour came in for lunch and turned on that radio, when suddenly there was the woman standing in front of him.

She was beaming broadly, everything in her manner suggesting they already knew each other. In fact it was only his natural shyness that stopped him greeting her. Then she placed a hand on his shoulder, as though he'd failed some test but was being forgiven anyway, and said:

'I was at your recital the other day. At San Lorenzo.'

'Thank you,' he replied, even as he realised how foolish this might sound. Then when the woman just went on beaming down at him, he said: 'Oh yes, the San Lorenzo church. That's correct. I did indeed give a recital there.'

The woman laughed, then suddenly seated herself in the chair in front of him. 'You say that like you've had a whole string of engagements lately,' she said, a hint of mockery in her voice.

'If that is so, I've given you a misleading impression. The recital you attended was my only one in two months.'

'But you're just starting out,' she said. 'You're doing fine to get any engagements at all. And that was a good crowd the other day.'

'A good crowd? There were only twenty-four people.'

'It was the afternoon. It was good for an afternoon recital.'

'I should not complain. Still, it wasn't a good crowd. Tourists with nothing better to do.'

'Oh! You shouldn't be so dismissive. After all, I was there. I was one of those tourists.' Then as he began to redden – for he hadn't meant to give offence – she touched his arm and said with a smile: 'You're just starting out. Don't worry about audience size. That's not why you're performing.'

'Oh? Then why am I performing if not for an audience?'

'That's not what I said. What I'm saying to you is that at this stage in your career, twenty in the audience or two hundred, it doesn't matter. Should I tell you why not? Because you've got it!'

'I have it?'

'You have it. Most definitely. You have . . . *potential.*'

He stifled a brusque laugh that came to his lips. He felt more reproach towards himself than for her, for he had expected her to say 'genius' or at least 'talent' and it immediately struck him how deluded he'd been to expect such a comment. But the woman was continuing:

'At this stage, what you're doing is waiting for that one person to come and hear you. And that one person might just as easily be in a room like that one on Tuesday, in a crowd of just twenty people . . .'

'There were twenty-four, not including the organisers . . .'

'Twenty-four, whatever. What I'm saying is that numbers don't matter right now. What matters is that one person.'

'You refer to the man from the recording company?'

'Recording? Oh no, no. That'll take care of itself. No, I mean the person who'll make you blossom. The person who'll hear you and realise you're not just another well-trained mediocrity. That even though you're still in your chrysalis, with just a little help, you'll emerge as a butterfly.'

'I see. By any chance, might you be this person?'

'Oh, come on! I can see you're a proud young man. But it doesn't look to me like you have so many mentors falling over themselves to get to you. At least not ones of my rank.'

It occurred to him then that he was in the midst of making a colossal blunder, and he considered the woman's features carefully. She'd now removed her sunglasses, and he could see a face that was essentially gentle and kind, yet with upset and perhaps anger not far away. He went on looking at her, hoping he'd soon recognise her, but in the end he was forced to say:

'I'm very sorry. You are perhaps a distinguished musician?'

'I'm Eloise McCormack,' she announced with a smile, and held out her hand. Unfortunately, the name meant nothing to Tibor and he found himself in a quandary. His first instinct was to feign astonishment, and he actually said: 'Really. This is quite amazing.' Then he pulled himself together, realising such bluffing was not only dishonest, but likely to lead to embarrassing exposure within seconds. So he sat up straight and said:

'Miss McCormack, it's an honour to meet you. I realise this will seem unbelievable to you, but I beg you to make allowances both for my youth and for the fact that I grew up in the former Eastern bloc, behind the Iron Curtain. There are many film stars and political personalities who are household names in the West, of whom, even today, I remain ignorant. So you must forgive me that I do not know precisely who you are.'

'Well . . . that's commendably frank.' Despite her words, she was clearly affronted, and her ebullience seemed to drain away. After an awkward moment, he said again:

'You are a distinguished musician, yes?'

She nodded, her gaze drifting across the square.

'Once again I must apologise,' he said. 'It was indeed an honour that someone like you should come to my recital. And may I ask your instrument?'

'Like you,' she said quickly. 'Cello. That's why I came in. Even if it's a humble little recital like yours, I can't help myself. I can't walk by. I have a sense of mission, I guess.'

'A mission?'

'I don't know what else to call it. I want all cellists to play well. To play beautifully. So often, they play in a misguided way.'

'Excuse me, but is it just we cellists who are guilty of this misguided performance? Or do you refer to all musicians?'

'Maybe the other instruments too. But I'm a cellist, so I listen to other cellists, and when I hear something going wrong . . . You know, the other day, I saw some young musicians playing in the lobby of the Museo Civico and people were just rushing past them, but I had to stop and listen. And you know, it was all I could do to stop myself going right up to them and telling them.'

[197]

'They were making errors?'

'Not errors exactly. But . . . well, it just wasn't there. It wasn't nearly there. But there you go, I ask too much. I know I shouldn't expect everyone to come up to the mark I set for myself. They were just music students, I guess.'

She leaned back in her seat for the first time and gazed at some children, over by the central fountain, noisily soaking one another. Eventually, Tibor said:

'You felt this urge also on Tuesday perhaps. The urge to come up to me and make your suggestions.'

She smiled, but then the next moment her face became very serious. 'I did,' she said. 'I really did. Because when I heard you, I could hear the way I once was. Forgive me, this is going to sound so rude. But the truth is, you're not quite on the correct path just now. And when I heard you, I so wanted to help you find it. Sooner rather than later.'

'I must point out, I have been tutored by Oleg Petrovic.' Tibor stated this flatly and waited for her response. To his surprise, he saw her trying to suppress a smile.

'Petrovic, yes,' she said. 'Petrovic, in his day, was a very respectable musician. And I know that to his students he must still appear a considerable figure. But to many of us now, his ideas, his whole approach . . .' She shook her head and spread out her hands. Then as Tibor, suddenly speechless with fury, continued to stare at her, she once again placed a hand on his arm. 'I've said enough. I've no right. I'll leave you in peace.'

She rose to her feet and this action soothed his anger; Tibor had a generous temperament and it wasn't in his nature to remain cross with people for long. Besides, what the woman had just said about his old teacher had struck an uncomfortable chord deep within him – thoughts he'd not quite dared to express to himself. So when he looked up at her, his face showed confusion more than anything else.

'Look,' she said, 'you're probably too angry with me just now to think about this. But I'd like to help you. If you do decide you want to talk this over, I'm staying over there. At the Excelsior.'

This hotel, the grandest in our city, stands at the opposite end of the square from the cafe, and she now pointed it out to Tibor, smiled, and began to walk off towards it. He was still watching her when she turned suddenly near the central fountain, startling some pigeons, gave him a wave, then continued on her way.

Over the next two days he found himself thinking about the encounter many times. He saw again the smirk around her mouth as he'd so proudly announced Petrovic's name and felt the anger rising afresh. But on reflection, he could see he had not really been angry on his old teacher's behalf. It was rather that he had become accustomed to the idea that Petrovic's name would always produce a certain impact, that it could be relied upon to induce attention and respect: in other words, he'd come to depend on it as a sort of certificate he could brandish around the world. What had so disturbed him was the possibility that this certificate didn't carry nearly the weight he'd supposed.

He kept remembering too her parting invitation, and during those hours he sat in the square, he found his gaze returning to the far end, and the grand entrance of the Excelsior Hotel, where a steady stream of taxis and limousines drew up in front of the doorman.

Finally, on the third day after his conversation with Eloise McCormack, he crossed the piazza, entered the marbled lobby and asked the front desk to call her extension. The receptionist spoke into the phone, asked his name, then after a short exchange, passed the receiver to him.

'I'm so sorry,' he heard her voice say. 'I forgot to ask you your name the other day and it took me a while to figure out who you were. But of course I haven't forgotten you. As a matter of fact, I've been thinking about you an awful lot. There's so much I'd like to talk through with you. But you know, we have to do this right. Do you have your cello? No, of course you don't. Why don't you come back in an hour, exactly one hour, and this time bring your cello. I'll be waiting here for you.'

When he returned to the Excelsior with his instrument, the receptionist immediately indicated the elevators and told him Miss McCormack was expecting him.

The idea of entering her room, even in the middle of the afternoon, had struck him as awkwardly intimate, and he was relieved to find a large suite, the bedroom closed off entirely from view. The tall French windows had boarded shutters, for the moment folded back, so the lace curtains moved in the breeze, and he could see that by stepping through onto the balcony, he'd find himself looking over the square. The room itself, with its rough stone walls and dark wood floor, had almost a monastic air about it, softened only partially by the flowers, cushions and antique furniture. She, in contrast, was dressed in T-shirt, tracksuit trousers and trainers, as though she'd just come in from running. She welcomed him with little ceremony – no offer of tea or coffee – and said to him:

'Play for me. Play me something you played at your recital.'

She had indicated a polished upright chair carefully placed in the centre of the room, so he sat down on it and unpacked his cello. Rather disconcertingly, she sat herself in front of one of the big windows so that he could see her almost exactly in profile, and she continued to stare into the space before her all the time he tuned up. Her posture didn't alter as he began to play, and when he came to the end of his first piece, she didn't say a word. So he moved quickly to another piece, and then another. A half-hour went by, then a whole hour. And something to do with the shaded room and its austere acoustics, the afternoon sunlight diffused by the drifting lace curtains, the background hubbub rising from the piazza, and above all, her presence, drew from him notes that held new depths, new suggestions. Towards the end of the hour, he was convinced he'd more than fulfilled her expectations, but when he had finished his last piece, and they had sat in silence for several moments, she at last turned in her chair towards him and said:

'Yes, I understand exactly where you are. It won't be easy, but you can do it. Definitely, you can do it. Let's start with the Britten. Play it again, just the first movement, and then we'll talk. We can work through this together, a little at a time.'

When he heard this, he felt an impulse just to pack away his instrument and leave. But then some other instinct – perhaps it was simply curiosity, perhaps something deeper – overcame his pride and compelled him to start playing again the piece she had requested. When after several bars she stopped him and began to talk, he again felt the urge to leave. He resolved, just out of politeness, to endure this uninvited tutorial for at most another five minutes. But he found himself staying a little longer, then longer again. He played some more, she talked again. Her words would always strike him initially as pretentious and far too abstract, but when he tried to accommodate their thrust into his playing, he was surprised by the effect. Before he realised, another hour had gone by.

'I could suddenly see something,' he explained to us. 'A garden I'd not yet entered. There it was, in the distance. There were things in the way. But for the first time, there it was. A garden I'd never seen before.'

The sun had almost set when he finally left the hotel, crossed the piazza to the cafe tables, and allowed himself the luxury of an almond cake with whipped cream, his sense of elation barely contained.

For the next several days, he returned to her hotel each afternoon and always came away, if not with the same sense of revelation he'd experienced on that first visit, then at least filled with fresh energy and hope. Her comments grew bolder, and to an outsider, had there been one, might have seemed presumptuous, but Tibor was no longer capable of regarding her interventions in such terms. His fear now was that her visit to the city would come to an end, and this thought began to haunt him, disturbing his sleep, and casting a shadow as he walked out into the square after another exhilarating session. But whenever he tentatively raised this question with her, the replies were always vague and far from reassuring. 'Oh, just until it gets too chilly for me,' she had said once. Or another time: 'I guess I'll stay as long as I'm not bored here.'

'But what's she like herself?' we kept asking him. 'On the cello. What's she like?'

The first time we raised this question, Tibor didn't answer us properly, just saying something like: 'She told me she was a virtuoso, right from the start,' then changing the subject. But when he realised we wouldn't let it go, he sighed and began to explain it to us.

The fact was, even at that first session, Tibor had been curious to hear her play, but had been too intimidated to ask her to do so. He'd felt only a tiny nudge of suspicion when, looking around her room, he'd seen no sign of her own cello. After all, it was perfectly natural she wouldn't bring a cello on holiday with her. And then again, it was possible there was an instrument – perhaps a rented one – in the bedroom behind the closed door.

But as he'd continued to return to the suite for further sessions, the suspicions had grown. He'd done his best to push them out of his mind, for by this time, he'd lost any lingering reservations about their meetings. The mere fact that she was listening to him seemed to draw fresh layers from his imagination, and in the hours between these afternoon sessions, he'd often find himself preparing a piece in his mind, anticipating her comments, her shakes of the head, her frown, the affirming nod, and most gratifying of all, those instances she became transported by a passage he was playing, when her eyes would close and her hands, almost against her will, began shadowing the movements he was making. All the same, the suspicions wouldn't go away, and then one day he came to the room and the bedroom door had been left ajar. He could see more stone walls, what looked to be a medieval four-poster bed, but no trace of a cello. Would a virtuoso, even on holiday, go so long without touching her instrument? But this question, too, he pushed out of his mind.

As the summer went on, they began to prolong their conversations by coming over to the cafe together after their sessions, and she'd buy him coffees, cakes, sometimes a sandwich. Now their talk was no longer just about music – though everything always seemed to come back to it. For instance, she might question him about the German girl he'd been close to in Vienna.

'But you must understand, she was never my girlfriend,' he would tell her. 'We were never like that.'

'You mean you never became physically intimate? That doesn't mean you weren't in love with her.'

'No, Miss Eloise, that is incorrect. I was fond of her, certainly. But we were not in love.'

'But when you played me the Rachmaninov yesterday, you were remembering an emotion. It was love, romantic love.'

'No, that is absurd. She was a good friend, but we did not love.'

'But you play that passage like it's the *memory* of love. You're so young, and yet you know desertion, abandonment. That's why you play that third movement the way you do. Most cellists, they play it with joy. But for you, it's not about joy, it's about the memory of a joyful time that's gone for ever.'

They had conversations like this, and he was often tempted to question her in return. But just as he'd never dared ask Petrovic a personal question in the whole time he'd studied under him, he now felt unable to ask anything of substance about her. Instead, he dwelt on the little things she let fall – how she now lived in Portland, Oregon, how she'd moved there from Boston three years ago, how she disliked Paris 'because of its sad associations' – but drew back from asking her to expand.

She would laugh much more easily now than in the first days of their friendship, and she developed the habit, when they stepped out of the Excelsior and crossed the piazza, of linking her arm through his. This was the point at which we first started noticing them, a curious couple, he looking so much younger than he actually was, she looking in some ways motherly, in other ways 'like a flirty actress', as Ernesto put it. In the days before we got to talking with Tibor, we used to waste a lot of idle chat on them, the way men in a band do. If they strolled past us, arm in arm, we'd look at each other and say: 'What do you think? They've been at it, yes?' But having enjoyed the speculation, we'd then shrug and admit it was unlikely: they just didn't have the atmosphere of lovers. And once we came to know Tibor, and he began telling us about those afternoons in her suite, none of us thought to tease him or make any funny suggestions.

Then one afternoon when they were sitting in the square with coffee and cakes, she began to talk about a man who wanted to marry her. His name was Peter Henderson and he ran a successful business in Oregon selling golfing equipment. He was smart, kind, well respected in the community. He was six years older than Eloise, but that was hardly old. There were two young children from his first marriage, but things had been settled amicably.

'So now you know what I'm doing here,' she said with a nervous laugh he'd never heard from her before. 'I'm hiding out. Peter has no idea where I am. I guess it's cruel of me. I called him last Tuesday, told him I was in Italy, but I didn't say which city. He was mad at me and I guess he's entitled to be.'

'So,' said Tibor. 'You are spending the summer contemplating your future.'

'Not really. I'm just hiding.'

'You do not love this Peter?'

She shrugged. 'He's a nice man. And I don't have a lot of other offers on the table.'

'This Peter. He is a music lover?'

'Oh . . . Where I live now, he would certainly count as one. After all, he goes to concerts. And afterwards, in the restaurant, he says a lot of nice things about what we just heard. So I guess he's a music lover.'

'But he . . . appreciates you?'

'He knows it won't always be easy, living with a virtuoso.' She gave a sigh. 'That's been the problem for me all my life. It won't be easy for you either. But you and me, we don't really have a choice. We have our paths to follow.'

She didn't bring Peter up again, but now, after that exchange, a new dimension had opened in their relationship. When she had those quiet moments of thought after he'd finished playing, or when, sitting together in the piazza, she became distant, staring off past the neighbouring parasols, there was nothing uncomfortable about it, and far from feeling ignored, he knew his presence there beside her was appreciated.

One afternoon when he'd finished playing a piece, she asked him to play again one short passage – just eight bars – from near the close. He did as asked and saw the little furrow remain on her forehead.

'That doesn't sound like us,' she said, shaking her head. As usual, she was sitting in profile to him in front of the big windows. 'The rest of what you played was good. All the rest of it, that *was* us. But that passage there . . .' She did a little shudder.

He played it again, differently, though not at all sure what he was aiming for, and wasn't surprised to see her shake her head again.

'I'm sorry,' he said. 'You must express yourself more clearly. I do not understand this "not us".'

'You mean you want me to play it myself? Is that what you're saying?'

She'd spoken calmly, but as she now turned to face him, he was aware of a tension descending on them. She was looking at him steadily, almost challengingly, waiting for his answer.

Eventually he said: 'No, I'll try again.'

'But you're wondering why I don't just play it myself, aren't you? Borrow your instrument and demonstrate what I mean.'

'No . . .' He shook his head with what he hoped looked like nonchalance. 'No. I think it works well, what we've always done. You suggest verbally, then I play. That way, it's not like I copy, copy, copy. Your words open windows for me. If you played yourself, the windows would not open. I'd only copy.'

She considered this, then said: 'You're probably right. Okay, I'll try and express myself a little better.'

And for the next few minutes she talked – about the distinction between epilogues and bridging passages. Then when he played those bars once more, she smiled and nodded approvingly.

But from that little exchange on, something shadowy had entered their afternoons. Perhaps it had been there all along, but now it was out of the bottle and hovered between them. Another time, when they were sitting in the piazza, he'd been telling her the story of how the previous owner of his cello had come by it in the Soviet Union days by bartering several pairs of American jeans. When he'd finished the story, she looked at him with a curious half-smile and said:

'It's a good instrument. It has a fine voice. But since I've never so much as touched it, I can't really judge it.'

He knew then she was again moving towards that territory, and he quickly looked away, saying:

'For someone of your stature, it would not be an adequate instrument. Even for me, now, it is barely adequate.'

He found he could no longer relax during a conversation with her for fear she would hijack it and bring it back onto this territory. Even during their most enjoyable exchanges, a part of his mind would have to remain on guard, ready to shut her off if she found yet another opening. Even so, he couldn't divert her every time, and he'd simply pretend not to hear when she said things like: 'Oh, it would be so much easier if I could just play it for you!'

Towards the end of September – there was now a chill in the breeze – Giancarlo received a phone call from Mr Kaufmann in Amsterdam; there was a vacancy for a cellist in a small chamber group at a five-star hotel in the centre of the city. The group played in a minstrels' gallery overlooking the dining room four evenings a week, and the musicians also had other 'light, non-musical duties' elsewhere in the hotel. Board and accommodation terms were available. Mr Kaufmann had immediately remembered Tibor and the post was being held open for him. We gave Tibor the news straight away – in the cafe the very evening of Mr Kaufmann's call – and I think we were all taken aback by the coolness of Tibor's response. It was certainly a contrast to his attitude earlier in the summer, when we'd fixed up his 'audition' with Mr Kaufmann. Giancarlo, in particular, became very angry.

'So what is it you have to think over so carefully?' he demanded of the boy. 'What were you expecting? Carnegie Hall?'

'I'm not ungrateful. Nevertheless, I must give this matter some thought. To play for people while they chat and eat. And these other hotel duties. Is this really suitable for someone like me?'

Giancarlo always lost his temper too quickly, and now the rest of us had to stop him from grabbing Tibor by his jacket and shouting into his face. Some of us even felt obliged to take the boy's side, pointing out it was his life, after all, and that he was under no obligation to take any job he was uncomfortable with. Things eventually calmed down, and Tibor then began to agree the job had some good points if viewed as a temporary measure. And our city, he pointed out rather insensitively, would become a backwater once the tourist season was over. Amsterdam at least was a cultural centre.

'I'll give this matter careful thought,' he said in the end. 'Perhaps you will kindly tell Mr Kaufmann I will give him my decision within three days.'

Giancarlo was hardly satisfied by this – he'd expected fawning gratitude, after all – but he went off all the same to call back Mr Kaufmann. During the whole of this discussion that evening, Eloise McCormack had not been mentioned, but it was clear to us all her influence was behind everything Tibor had been saying.

'That woman's turned him into an arrogant little shit,' Ernesto said after Tibor had left. 'Let him take that attitude with him to Amsterdam. He'll soon get a few corners knocked off him.'

Tibor had never told Eloise about his audition with Mr Kaufmann. He'd been on the verge of doing so many times, but had always drawn back, and the deeper their friendship had grown, the more it seemed a betrayal that he'd ever agreed to such a thing. So naturally Tibor felt no inclination to consult Eloise about these latest developments, or even allow her any inkling of them. But he'd never been good at concealment, and this decision to keep a secret from her had unexpected results.

It was unusually warm that afternoon. He'd come to the hotel as usual, and begun to play for her some new pieces he'd been preparing. But after barely three minutes, she made him stop, saying:

'There's something wrong. I thought it when you first came in. I know you so well now, Tibor, I could tell, almost from the way you knocked on the door. Now I've heard you play, I know for certain. It's useless, you can't hide it from me.'

He was in some dismay, and lowering his bow, was about to make a clean breast of everything, when she put up her hand and said:

'This is something we can't keep running away from. You always try to avoid it, but it's no use. I want to discuss it. The whole of this past week, I've been wanting to discuss it.'

'Really?' He looked at her in astonishment.

'Yes,' she said, and moved her chair so that for the first time she was directly facing him. 'I never intended to deceive you, Tibor. These last few weeks, they haven't been the easiest for me, and you've been such a dear friend. I'd so hate it if you thought I ever meant to play some cheap trick on you. No, please, don't try and stop me this time. I want to say this. If you gave me that cello right now and asked me to play, I'd have to say no, I can't do it. Not because the instrument isn't good enough, nothing like that. But if you're now thinking I'm a fake, that I've somehow pretended to be something I'm not, then I want to tell you you're mistaken. Look at everything we've achieved together. Isn't that proof enough I'm no fake anything? Yes, I told you I was a virtuoso. Well, let me explain what I meant by that. What I meant was that I was born with a very special gift, just as you were. You and me, we have something most other cellists will never have, no matter how hard they practise. I was able to recognise it in you, the moment I first heard you in that church. And in some way, you must have recognised it in me too. That's why you decided to come to this hotel that first time.

'There aren't many like us, Tibor, and we recognise each other. The fact that I've not yet learned to play the cello doesn't really change anything. You have to understand, I *am* a virtuoso. But I'm one who's yet to be *unwrapped*. You too, you're still not entirely unwrapped, and that's what I've been doing these past few weeks. I've been trying to help you shed those layers. But I never tried to deceive you. Ninety-nine per cent of cellists, there's nothing there under those layers, there's nothing to unwrap. So people like us, we have to help each other. When we see each other in a crowded square, wherever, we have to reach out for one another, because there are so few of us.'

He noticed that tears had appeared in her eyes, but her voice had remained steady. She now fell silent and turned away from him again.

'So you believe yourself to be a special cellist,' he said

after a moment. 'A virtuoso. The rest of us, Miss Eloise, we have to take our courage in our hands and we unwrap ourselves, as you put it, all the time unsure what we will find underneath. Yet you, you do not care for this unwrapping. You do nothing. But you are so sure you are this virtuoso . . .'

'Please don't be angry. I know it sounds a little crazy. But that's how it is, it's the truth. My mother, she recognised my gift straight away, when I was tiny. I'm grateful to her for that at least. But the teachers she found for me, when I was four, when I was seven, when I was eleven, they were no good. Mom didn't know that, but I did. Even as a small girl, I had this instinct. I knew I had to protect my gift against people who, however well-intentioned they were, could completely destroy it. So I shut them out. You've got to do the same, Tibor. Your gift is precious.'

'Forgive me,' Tibor interrupted, now more gently. 'You say you played the cello as a child. But today . . .'

'I haven't touched the instrument since I was eleven. Not since the day I explained to Mom I couldn't continue with Mr Roth. And she understood. She agreed it was much better to do nothing and wait. The crucial thing was not to damage my gift. My day may still come though. Okay, sometimes I think I've left it too late. I'm forty-one years old now. But at least I haven't damaged what I was born with. I've met so many teachers over the years who've said they'd help me, but I saw through them. Sometimes it's difficult to tell, Tibor, even for us. These teachers, they're so . . . *professional*, they talk so well, you listen and at first you're fooled. You think, yes, at last, someone to help me, he's one of *us*. Then you realise he's nothing of the kind. And that's when you have to be tough and shut yourself off. Remember that, Tibor, it's always better to wait. Sometimes I feel bad about it, that I still haven't unveiled my gift. But I haven't damaged it, and that's what counts.'

He eventually played for her a couple of the pieces he'd prepared, but they couldn't retrieve their usual mood and they ended the session early. Down in the piazza, they drank their coffee, speaking little, until he told her of his plans to leave the city for a few days. He'd always wanted to explore the surrounding countryside, he said, so now he'd arranged a short holiday for himself.

'It'll do you good,' she said quietly. 'But don't stay away too long. We still have a lot to do.'

He reassured her he'd be back within a week at the most. Nevertheless, there was still something uneasy in her manner as they parted.

He'd not been entirely truthful about his going away: he hadn't yet made any arrangements. But after leaving Eloise that afternoon, he went home and made several phone calls, eventually reserving a bed at a youth hostel in the mountains near the Umbrian border. He came to see us at the cafe that night, and as well as telling us about his trip – we gave him all kinds of conflicting advice about where to go and what to see – he rather sheepishly asked Giancarlo to let Mr Kaufmann know he'd like to take up the job offer.

'What else can I do?' he said to us. 'By the time I get back, I'll have no money left at all.'

*

Tibor had a pleasant enough break in our countryside. He didn't tell us much about it, other than that he'd made friends with some German hikers, and that he'd spent more than he could afford in the hillside trattorias. He came back after a week, looking visibly refreshed, but anxious to establish that Eloise McCormack had not left the city during his absence.

The tourist crowds were beginning to thin by then, and the cafe waiters were bringing out terrace heaters to place among the outdoor tables. On the afternoon of his return, at their usual time, Tibor took his cello to the Excelsior again, and was pleased to discover not only that Eloise was there waiting for him, but that she'd obviously missed him. She welcomed him with emotion, and just as someone else, in a surfeit of affection, might have plied him with food or drink, she pushed him into his usual chair and began impatiently unpacking the cello, saying: 'Play for me! Come on! Just play!'

They had a wonderful afternoon together. He'd worried beforehand how things would be, after her 'confession' and the way they'd last parted, but all the tension seemed simply to have evaporated, and the atmosphere between them felt better than ever. Even when, after he'd finished a piece, she closed her eyes and embarked on a long, stringent critique of his performance, he felt no resentment, only a hunger to understand her as fully as possible. The next day and the day after, it was the same: relaxed, at times even jokey, and he felt sure he'd never played better in his life. They didn't allude at all to that conversation before he'd gone away, nor did she ask about his break in the countryside. They only talked about the music.

Then on the fourth day after his return, a series of small mishaps – including a leaking toilet cistern in his room – prevented him going to the Excelsior at the usual hour. By the time he came past the cafe, the light was fading, the waiters had lit the candles inside the little glass bowls, and we were a couple of numbers into our dinner set. He waved to us, then went on across the square towards the hotel, his cello making him look like he was limping.

He noticed the receptionist hesitate slightly before phoning up to her. Then when she opened the door, she greeted him warmly, but somehow differently, and before he had a chance to speak, she said quickly:

'Tibor, I'm so glad you've come. I was just telling Peter everything about you. That's right, Peter's found me at last!' Then she called into the room: 'Peter, he's here! Tibor's here. And with his cello too!'

As Tibor stepped into the room, a large, shambling, greying man in a pale polo shirt rose to his feet with a smile. He gripped Tibor's hand very firmly and said: 'Oh, I've heard all about you. Eloise is convinced you're gonna be a big star.'

'Peter's persistent,' she was saying. 'I knew he'd find me in the end.'

'No hiding from me,' said Peter. Then he was pulling up a chair for Tibor, pouring him a glass of champagne from an ice-bucket on the cabinet. 'Come on, Tibor, help us celebrate our reunion.'

Tibor sipped the champagne, aware that Peter had pulled up for him, by chance, his usual 'cello chair'. Eloise had vanished somewhere, and for a while, Tibor and Peter made conversation, their glasses in their hands. Peter seemed kindly and asked a lot of questions. How had it been for Tibor growing up in a place like Hungary? Had it been a shock when he'd first come to the West?

'I'd love to play an instrument,' Peter said. 'You're so lucky. I'd like to learn. A little late now though, I guess.'

'Oh, you can never say too late,' Tibor said.

'You're right. Never say too late. Too late is always just an excuse. No, the truth is, I'm a busy man, and I tell myself I'm too busy to learn French, to learn an instrument, to read *War and Peace*. All the things I've always wanted to do. Eloise used to play when she was a kid. I guess she told you about that.'

'Yes, she did. I understand she has a lot of natural gifts.'

'Oh, she sure does. Anyone who knows her will be able to see that. She has such sensitivity. She's the one who should be having those lessons. Me, I'm just Mr Banana Fingers.' He held up his hands and laughed. 'I'd like to play piano, but what can you do with hands like these? Great for digging the earth, that's what my people did for generations. But that lady' – he indicated towards the door with his glass – 'now she's got sensitivity.'

Eventually, Eloise emerged from the bedroom in a dark evening dress and a lot of jewellery.

'Peter, don't bore Tibor,' she said. 'He's not interested in golf.'

Peter held out his hands and looked pleadingly at Tibor. 'Now tell me, Tibor. Did I say a single word to you about golf?'

Tibor said he should be going; that he could see he was keeping the couple from their dinner. This was met by protests from both of them, and Peter said:

'Now look at me. Do I look like I'm dressed for dinner?'

And though Tibor thought he looked perfectly decent, he gave the laugh that seemed expected of him. Then Peter said:

'You can't leave without playing something. I've been hearing so much about your playing.'

Confused, Tibor had actually started to unfasten his cello case, when Eloise said firmly, some new quality in her voice:

'Tibor's right. Time's getting on. The restaurants in this town, they don't keep your table if you don't come on time. Peter, you get yourself dressed. Maybe a shave too? I'll see Tibor out. I want to speak with him in private.'

In the lift, they smiled affectionately at each other, but didn't speak. When they came outside, they found the piazza lit up for the night. Local kids, back from their holidays, were kicking balls, or chasing each other around the fountain. The evening *passeggiata* was in full flow, and I suppose our music would have come drifting through the air to where they were standing.

'Well, that's it,' she said, eventually. 'He's found me, so I guess he deserves me.'

'He is a most charming person,' Tibor said. 'You intend to return to America now?'

'In a few days. I suppose I will.'

'You intend to marry?'

'I guess so.' For an instant, she looked at him earnestly, then looked away. 'I guess so,' she said again.

'I wish you much happiness. He is a kind man. Also a music lover. That's important for you.'

'Yes. That's important.'

'When you were getting ready just now. We were talking not of golf, but of music lessons.'

'Oh really? You mean for him or for me?'

'For both. However, I don't suppose there will be many teachers in Portland, Oregon, who could teach you.'

She gave a laugh. 'Like I said, it's difficult for people like us.'

'Yes, I appreciate that. After these last few weeks, I appreciate that more than ever.' Then he added: 'Miss Eloise, there is something I must tell you before we part. I will soon leave for Amsterdam, where I have been given a position in a large hotel.'

'You're going to be a porter?'

'No. I will play in a small chamber group in the hotel dining room. We will entertain the hotel guests while they eat.'

He was watching her carefully and saw something ignite behind her eyes, then fade away. She laid a hand on his arm and smiled.

'Well then, good luck.' Then she added: 'Those hotel guests. They've got some treat coming up.'

'I hope so.'

For another moment, they remained standing there together, just beyond the pool of light cast by the front of the hotel, the bulky cello between them.

'And I hope also', he said, 'you'll be very happy with Mr Peter.'

'I hope so too,' she said and laughed again. Then she kissed him on the cheek and gave him a quick hug. 'You take care of yourself,' she said.

Tibor thanked her, then before he quite realised it, he was watching her walking back towards the Excelsior.

Tibor left our city soon after that. The last time we had drinks with him, he was clearly very grateful to Giancarlo and Ernesto for his job, and to us all for our friendship, but I couldn't help getting the impression he was being a little aloof with us. A few of us thought this, not just me, though Giancarlo, typically, now took Tibor's side, saying the boy had just been feeling excited and nervous about this next step in his life.

'Excited? How can he be excited?' Ernesto said. 'He's spent the summer being told he's a genius. A hotel job, it's a comedown. Sitting talking to us, that's a comedown too. He was a nice kid at the start of the summer. But after what that woman's done to him, I'm glad we're seeing the back of him.'

Like I said, this all happened seven years ago. Giancarlo, Ernesto, all the boys from that time except me and Fabian, they've all moved on. Until I spotted him in the piazza the other day, I hadn't thought about our young Hungarian maestro for a long time. He wasn't so hard to recognise. He'd put on weight, certainly, and was looking a lot thicker around the neck. And the way he gestured with his finger, calling for a waiter, there was something – maybe I imagined this – something of the impatience, the off-handedness that comes with a certain kind of bitterness. But maybe that's unfair. After all, I only glimpsed him. Even so, it seemed to me he'd lost that youthful anxiety to please, and those careful manners he had back then. No bad thing in this world, you might say.

I would have gone over and talked with him, but by the end of our set he'd already gone. For all I know, he was here only for the afternoon. He was wearing a suit – nothing very grand, just a regular one – so perhaps he has a day job now behind a desk somewhere. Maybe he had some business to do nearby and came through our city just for old times' sake, who knows? If he comes back to the square, and I'm not playing, I'll go over and have a word with him.